ROTTEN TOMMY

A HORROR NOVEL

DAVID SODERGREN

This book is a work of fiction.
Any resemblance to names and people, living or dead, is purely coincidental.
No part of this publication may be reproduced or transmitted in any form without written permission from the author.

Copyright © 2024
All rights reserved.
ISBN-13: 9798320720029

For Heather
Couldn't have done it without ya!

PART I

1

1984

William Oliver Pratt *hated* children.

From their whining voices and garish clothes to their inability to use a handkerchief, William regarded children as loathsome vermin to be, at best, tolerated. So quite why he had been selected as head of Golden Thistle TV's children's department was a mystery that would forever elude him.

Since his humble beginnings in the industry, William had risen steadily through the ranks, promotion following promotion as surely as summer followed spring, until the untimely demise of the esteemed Reg Brooker led to his current — and greatly despised — position.

God, he oversaw some astonishing rubbish.

While his contemporaries in London were busying themselves with high-calibre series such as *Play For Today* and *Armchair Theatre,* he was producing lowest common denominator crap like *The Gum Tum Gang* and *Bobby's Magic Turnip*.

"*Puppets*," his new boss had said to him, as he chewed on a cigar over after-work brandies. "*Children* adore *puppets*." William had smiled and nodded at such sage advice, his fingers tightening into fists below the table. Puppets were the only thing he hated more than children. "*And don't forget the songs,*" Golden Thistle's chairman had continued, pausing a moment to allow William to bask in the glow of such wisdom. "*The children love a good song.*"

And so it was that William Oliver Pratt put on hold his desire to create prestige television in England's glorious capital city, and moved up north to the armpit of the United Kingdom, a miserable place the locals referred to as *Scotland*. Doing his best to ignore the weather and the incomprehensible accent, William immediately set to work, watching countless hours of tripe like *Rainbow* and *Button Moon* in a bid to see what his rivals were up to. Of course, those shows were produced by London's Thames Television, and Golden Thistle couldn't hope to compete financially. The allocated budgets were minuscule, and so William's big idea — his only idea, truth be told — had been to pump all the money into a single series. Quality, not quantity, was his philosophy... well, for everything outside the bedroom.

Entrusting the full autumn/winter budget to Quintin Horsham-Blake had seemed a prudent move. Quintin, an old chum from boarding school, had worked for the BBC, and knew how to bring in a show on time without sacrificing his artistic integrity.

Or so William had thought, until one week ago, when communication with Quintin broke down. Without a word, filming had halted on Golden Thistle's flagship series, *Rumplejack*. The cast and crew were apparently sent home without anyone informing him, despite the fact he was still paying their hotel bills, and not a peep had been heard from anyone involved in the production for days. Unable to reach Quintin on the telephone, William had — on the instruction of the chairman — made the treacherous drive from Glasgow to pay the errant director a visit, and possibly knock some sense into him.

"Bloody unprofessional," he muttered to himself, as he stalked angrily down the path towards the secluded cottage he had rented for the director. What reason could the man have to halt production? Did he need the money for gambling debts? Were the actors causing him bother? Or were the Scottish crew proving too slovenly and drunken to function?

Mud squelched beneath his shoes, the rain pattering lightly off his tweed suit. William glanced at the spindly limbed trees that lined the path, and wondered what terrors lurked beyond them. God, he hated the countryside, almost as much as he hated children and puppets. The sooner he could retrieve his money and drive back to Glasgow, the better. He didn't want to spend another second here, and work had to resume on *Rumplejack* with haste to prepare it for broadcast in March.

The cottage windows were shuttered, and no light escaped through the gaps. Perhaps Quintin wasn't home? Nonsense. His car was parked by the gate, and very poorly too, as if the man had been in a frightful hurry.

William climbed the uneven stone steps that led to the door, and knocked three times as he sheltered from the rain beneath the porch awning.

"Quintin? It's Pratt. William Pratt."

He waited as long as he could stand, but William was

anything but a patient man. He knocked again, louder this time.

"Quintin Horsham-Blake, I know you're in there! Let me in this instant, or I'll have the bloody police round here faster than—"

The door opened.

It was the smell that hit him first, the kind of malodorous stench he would expect from a council estate, or somewhere equally insalubrious. The interior was cloaked in darkness, and he squinted through the doorway. Was someone—

"Get in then," a voice hissed at him.

"Quintin?"

"Fucking *get in!*"

A hand, stained and dirty, extended from the black void, gripping his arm and hauling him over the threshold. William stumbled inside, the door slamming shut.

"What the *devil* is the meaning of this?" he seethed. "Put the bloody lights on, man! You're hardly living a pauper's existence, particularly when you've absconded with my—"

"Keep your voice down!"

One thing William detested — along with children, puppets, and the countryside — was being interrupted. "Don't use that tone with me, Quintin." He paused. "Switch the lights on, would you? This is a foolish way to behave."

He listened to Quintin's laboured breathing. "Did you see anyone... outside?" the man asked.

"Pardon? I asked you to put the lights on. I refuse to have a conversation in darkness like it's the bloody blackouts."

"Did you *see* anyone out there?" Quintin insisted. "It's a simple question. Answer it."

William bristled at the impertinence. "No, I *damn* well did not. Now, for the last time, will you—"

A *click,* and the dim glow of a table lamp partially illuminated the room.

"There. Happy now?"

William cast his eyes around the cottage. It was in a state of disrepair. Chairs and tables had been dismantled, the parts crudely affixed to the walls to cover the windows. Detritus littered the wooden floor, and the sofa had been shoved in front of the only other exit. But it was Quintin himself who shocked him the most. The man, who William knew to be of impeccable taste and grooming, looked like he had been found at a crime scene. His clothes were dirty — Quintin was the source of the foul odour, he surmised — and his hair was lank. He sported a scruffy beard, and his eyes, which once had sparkled with wit and intelligence, looked sunken and grey. The man was clearly ill, but that wasn't the worst of it.

That dubious honour fell to the blood that coated his face and clothes.

"My God," said William. "What happened here?"

"Keep the door locked night and day," the director whispered, with a knowing smile that caused flakes of dried blood to flutter from his cheeks. "Are you quite sure you didn't see anyone? Anyone... unusual?"

William could only shake his head.

Quintin fixed him with a glare. "Nobody? In the forest, perhaps watching through the trees?"

"I told you, I didn't see—"

"But are you *sure?*" The director stepped closer, and William noticed with alarm the metal fireplace poker in Quintin's hand. "It's *important!*"

"There's no one out there," he replied calmly. "You have my word. Now, do you need me to take you to hospital? You seem... poorly."

"I'm fine. I just have to keep the door locked night and day."

"Yes, that's, uh, sound advice." What to do? William had been prepared for an argument, for harsh words to be spoken... but not for this. The man had lost his mind. No wonder the production had fallen apart. "Look, I really do think you should see someone."

Quintin turned away. Was he even listening? He shuffled over to the windows, testing the strength of the wood. "Keep the door locked. But what about the windows? The song doesn't say anything about the windows!"

"Pull yourself together, man," said William in his most authoritative tone, the kind he usually reserved for women. "I suggest you seek professional help, and urgently. But for the time being, your private health issues do not concern me. You know why I'm here, Quintin. What's going on with the show? What's the status on Rumple—"

The director threw himself forwards, shoving William against the wall. His filthy, bloodstained fingers squirmed into William's mouth, squeezing down on his tongue.

"Quiet! Don't you listen, you stupid bastard? I said keep your voice down *or he'll hear you!*"

William — who excelled at verbal debates, but was less sure of himself in physical altercations — froze, waiting for Quintin to slide the crusted digits out of his mouth. The taste made him gag, and the violation shamed him.

"You," he blustered, "have just made the biggest mistake of your life. I'll see you never work again. I'll see your name in the papers as a liar and a charlatan and a... a bloody hoodwinker! And lastly, my good man, I'll take you to court and—"

The metal poker struck William in the stomach,

knocking the air from him. Gasping, he slid down the wall and landed heavily on his posterior.

"Oh shit, oh fuck," said Quintin, his gaze darting around the room. "I warned you, didn't I? I asked you... I *begged* you to keep quiet." There was panic in his voice. Panic, and total terror. *"He's here."*

William tried to rise, but the blow from the poker had hurt him. He blinked, and tears rolled down his cheeks as Quintin paced back and forth, clutching the fearsome weapon with both hands.

"Do you have a gun?" he asked.

William looked up at him in bewilderment. "A... a what?"

"A gun! A pistol, a rifle, a fucking bazooka! Anything!"

"You're mad. You're completely stark-raving mad. And to think I trusted you with my money."

Quintin turned on the spot, the poker trembling in his hands. "There... in the corner." His voice dropped to a whisper. "Do you see him?"

William snorted. "Absolutely blimmin' mad."

"Please," said Quintin. "Leave me be."

"Who *are* you talking to?"

"Don't you see him?"

"See who?" William squinted at the corner. "There's nobody here but you and I."

"He's right there!"

"Quintin, you've had a shock, and I'm going to alert the authorities. But before I do, I need to know what you've done with the money."

The director backed away, stumbling over broken furniture. "Don't you see him?"

"Where's the money, Quintin?"

"Leave me alone!" the director roared at nothing.

"Quintin! My money! Where is it?"

The director hit the wall. He could go no further. He glanced at William, his red eyes pleading, tears scything through dried blood. "You really don't see him?"

"Enough of this nonsense!" William pushed himself up from the floor, wincing at the residual pain. "Where is the budget from *Rumple*—"

"Don't say it!"

"—*jack?*"

Quintin shrieked, and raised the poker, holding it inches from his left eyeball. "You bastard!" he cried, and jerked the metal tool forwards. The tip plunged into his eye socket, annihilating the juicy orb.

"What are you doing?" asked William, rooted to the spot in shock.

Quintin twisted the implement, a freakish grimace plastered to his face as metal scraped loudly against bone, dark blood weeping from the ruptured socket. "You won't get me! If I can't see you, you won't—"

The poker flew from his hands, shooting across the room and embedding itself in the wall as if propelled by an invisible force.

"No!" screamed Quintin. He collapsed to the floor, crawling towards William, ragged flaps of skin dangling from his eye-socket as vile, soupy liquid spilled from the ruined crater, leaving a wet trail of revulsion. "Keep the door locked night and day, keep the door locked night and day, keep the door locked—" He stopped, and stared at William with his one remaining eye. "It's your fault!" he roared, and reached for his eye, lifting the lid, pulling it as far as it would stretch. With his other hand, he pressed his thumb and forefinger into the socket, forcing his fingertips under the lid until he pinched his eyeball like an olive.

With a scream, he squeezed.

The eyeball popped between his fingers, vomit spilling from his lips as he tore the remains free, wiping the sticky residue on the floor before turning to William with two ghastly, bleeding holes in his face.

"Keep the door locked night and day," he said. "Keep the door locked night and day, keep the door locked night and day, keep the door locked night and day, keep the door locked night and day, keep the door locked night and day, keep the—"

He was still chanting the words when William barged open the front door and ran from the cottage, the rain pounding against his face as he staggered into the night, unable to forget the look of horror on Quintin's face seconds before he had plunged a fire poker into his own eye. The funny thing was... at that moment, the man hadn't *looked* mad.

In fact, he had looked frighteningly sane.

40 YEARS LATER

keep the dooR locked night and day, keep the dOor locked nighT and day, keep ThE door locked Night and day, keep the dooR locked night and day, keep the dOor locked nighT and day, keep The door locked night and day, keEp the door locked Night and day, keep the dooR locked night and day, keep the doOr locked nighT and day, keep the door locked nighT and day, kEep the door locked Night and day, keep the dooR locked night and day, keep the dOor locked nighT and day, keep The door lockEd Night and day, so Tommy can't—

2

What annoys a noisy otter?

Becky Sharp knew the answer.

A noise annoys a noisy otter.

She knew, because the childhood riddle had been rattling around inside her head for the last four hours, ever since the builders had arrived at nine on the dot to resume work on the house. The men were pleasant enough, and she appreciated their work ethic, but 'quiet' was an alien concept to them.

She stared at the open document on her laptop.

What annoys a noisy otter, was all she had typed, over and over. She deleted the text.

A noise annoys a noisy otter.

It wasn't the builders' fault. They were only doing their job, one that she and John were paying them to do. An extension to the house, so her husband could have a ground floor office space in which to store all the files and folders and junk he used in his boring bank job. She didn't mean to be dismissive of his work; John often said the same. It *was* boring. But it paid well, and allowed her to pursue her own dream of being a screenwriter, an attempt to follow in the showbiz footsteps of her mother without the unwanted attention of being an actress.

"Fucking hell, that Haaland, eh?"

"Aye, no too shabby on the baw, is he?"

The men had stopped drilling or sawing or sanding, reverting to the classic sports banter she had become accustomed to over the last few days. Was it better than the industrial noise? She wasn't sure. Rolling a ball of Blu-tak over the tabletop, she leaned back in her chair, listening to the satisfying groan of the wood. Should she offer them some coffee? She knew the answer to that one. She *definitely* should. It was the polite thing to do. But the idea of walking through and interrupting them, of saying something stupid and having them laugh... no, she would stay put for now. If they wanted a hot drink, they knew where to find the kitchen.

God, they probably thought she was a right weirdo, holed up in the living room beneath a blanket and staring at a blank page on her laptop.

What annoys a noisy otter?

"Oh, shut up," she grumbled to herself.

Her temples throbbed, signalling the beginning of a headache. What time was it? Half-one? Surely they would break for lunch soon and bless her with a few precious moments of peace.

Then the drilling or sawing or sanding resumed, and Becky closed her eyes, secure in the knowledge she would achieve nothing today. Maybe she could go away for a few days? Brightening at the thought, she opened her browser and searched for weekend breaks in the Highlands. Somewhere remote, with only her laptop and some books, where she could sit in a lodge with a lochside view and just *write*.

The idea sounded heavenly. No one to bother her, no one to annoy her.

A noise annoys a noisy otter.

John wouldn't mind. He always encouraged her to take some time off.

A screeching whine erupted nearby. What the hell were those workmen up to now? Her foot tapped restlessly off the floor, and she got up and crossed the room, picking up her cigarettes and heading for the front door. No, wait. She would pass them if she went that way. Better to go to the back garden, via the kitchen, to avoid any awkward exchanges.

She slipped silently down the hall and entered the kitchen.

"Awright, Mrs Sharp?"

Damn it.

A workman was there already. She smiled politely. "Hello."

"No' too noisy for ye?"

"Nope."

"Just makin' the boys some tea. You want some?"

He was blocking the way to the back door.

"I'll be okay. Thank you, though."

He remained steadfast. "Making some good progress."

Now, here was a promising development! "Oh, really? Think you'll be finished early?"

He laughed as if she'd made a joke, and said, "You smoke?"

"What?" She looked down at the cigarette between her fingers. "Oh. Yes, I smoke."

"Didn't realise. I'd join you, but the boys are thirsty. You know what it's like, eh?"

"Yeah, I know what it's like," she said, puzzling over his words. What *what's* like?

"Next time."

"Yes... next time." She moved forwards, and he let her pass. By the time she made it outside, she *needed* a smoke. Christ, she was usually better at small talk than that. But she hadn't been ready, hadn't been prepared. The constant noise played havoc with her thoughts, and having strangers in her house unsettled her.

They're nice men, she thought. *And once they're finished, everything will be back to normal.*

She lit her cigarette and took a draw. Winter was fast approaching, and the air nipped at her bare arms, but it was good to be outside. She should do it more often. And she would, when there was more time. She and John could take a drive out to Beecraigs Country Park, or the Pentland Hills. They often spoke of going for a walk in the country, but John was so busy, even at weekends, and finding the time—

A knock at the window made her jump.

"Jesus, fuck," she said, turning to the window, where one of the builders was gesturing at her. Confused, she pointed at her cigarette. The man shook his head, jerking his thumb over his shoulder. What did *that* mean? Was someone behind her? She glanced over her own shoulder, then back to the window, but the man was gone.

"What the fuck does he want?" she mumbled, before the workman's outline appeared at the frosted glass of the back door.

"Here, Mrs Sharp," he said, as he opened the door. "You gotta see this."

"I'm... I'm smoking. Can it wait?"

"Can it fuck!" He looked embarrassed. "Ah, sorry about

the language, but you really should see this. We found something."

"What do you mean?"

What did she *think* he meant?

Even the builder seemed to be growing weary of the conversation. "In the wall. We found something hidden in the wall." He paused, letting the words sink in. "You'll want to see."

Becky extinguished her cigarette and followed the workman through the kitchen and hallway and into what had once been the living room. Now, with the furniture removed and replaced by foldaway chairs and a plastic table, and tools scattered across the floor, it felt more akin to a workshop. The most glaring omission was the enormous bookcase that had taken up the entire back wall. It had housed not only Becky's book collection, but her trinkets and souvenirs and plush toys. It made her sad to enter the room and not see it there. But with the unit temporarily absent, she noticed something new.

A hole in the wall, large enough to fit a small dog. The surrounding plaster was broken, and splinters of wood sprinkled the tarpaulin that covered the floor.

"That's where we found it," the workman said. "Right in there."

Becky walked to the hole and inspected it, tracing her finger around the perimeter. A gust of stale air seeped out like pus from a wound. Bracing herself, she peered inside. It was empty.

"What did you find?"

"*That.*"

Becky turned, unsure what to expect. Her mind raced. Gold bullions? A skeleton? The Ark of the Covenant?

"Oh," she said, as the decidedly less thrilling truth was revealed.

It was a box, roughly the size of two hardback books, and held shut by a brass latch. It reminded her of a pirate's treasure chest. Maybe it *was* full of gold bullions!

"What's inside?"

"Dunno. We were waiting for you."

"Thank you," she said, and she meant it. Her natural aversion to socialisation gave way to curiosity, and she picked the chest up. It smelt of old, damp wood.

"Go on, then. Open it."

She forced the rusted latch and popped the lid. A strange smell escaped, like the worm-ridden stench of an exhumed coffin. Inside, something was wrapped in crumpled plastic.

It was a Woolworths carrier bag.

"Shite, remember Woolies?" asked one of the men. "That closed about twenty years ago."

Becky was only half-listening. She peeled back the bag, revealing a stiff parchment wrapped around…

"Huh," she said, as three videotapes slid out from their paper wrapping. A chill skated down her spine, and she couldn't understand why.

"Videos?" The workman elbowed his friend. "Wee Mikey won't even know what they are!"

"Ah ken videos," the young man protested. "Ah've seen 'em on TikTok." He looked expectantly at Becky. All of them did. "So? What's oan them?"

"I'm not sure." She looked closely at the tapes. They had no sleeves, and on two of them, the label had been peeled off, leaving nothing but white residue. "The stickers have been scratched off. Wait…"

The same fate had almost befallen the third and last tape, but the ink had leaked through, branding a single word into the plastic.

"Rumplejack," she said. "What does that mean?"

Whatever Rumplejack was, the workmen unanimously agreed they had never heard of it. "Must be shite if none o' us have seen it," said Mikey.

"Rumplejack," mused another man. "Sounds like Scrumpy Jack. That's a cider, innit?"

Becky wasn't sure what to do with that information.

"Here," the man continued. "You got a video player?"

She shook her head, running her fingertips over the tapes. Then, without another word, she left the room. As she did so, she heard the men talking, their voices lowered.

"She's a funny one, eh?"

"Aye. No' even a goodbye."

She placed the cassettes on the kitchen table and washed her hands to rid them of the antique stink. Once dry, she turned her attention back to the tapes. Such an odd find. In *her* house, in *her* wall. How long had they been there?

The kitchen door opened, and a workman entered. "You dropped this, love." He offered her the piece of paper the tapes had been wrapped in. "There's something on it."

Becky took the paper, handling it delicately lest the weathered parchment crumble in her hands, and laid it flat on the table.

MISSING was written across the top in bold print, above a black-and-white photo of a little girl. The child wore a serious and unsmiling expression, her hair tied back. There were more words beneath the picture, but Becky's mind refused to process the meaningless jumble of symbols.

"Might be nothing," the builder said, sounding distant. "But I thought you'd like to see."

"Yes, thank you," she said distractedly.

"Mean anything to you?"

"Huh?"

"The girl on the poster. Do you know her?"

"No." She smiled with great effort. "I don't know her." The man remained in the kitchen. What did he want? "Thank you," she said, hoping that would be enough.

With a cheery grin, he said, "No worries," and finally left.

Only once she was alone did Becky look at the poster again. She stared at it, right into the eyes of the little girl.

MISSING.

Do you know her, the man had asked, and she had lied to him, lied to his face. This girl was instantly recognisable to her. She recalled the unsmiling face from portraits that had once hung on the walls of this very house, and forgotten photographs that gathered dust in mouldy photo albums in the attic. She touched the paper, caressing the creased, yellowing image.

"It's me," she said to herself, a curious pit opening up in her stomach. "It's fucking *me.*"

3

When John arrived home, Becky was seated in the kitchen, feverishly scrolling on her laptop. The builders were gone, though she hadn't noticed them leave. She looked up at her husband.

"I didn't expect you home so early."

He offered a half-smile that said, *oh boy, here we go again.* "Becky, I'm two hours *late*. What time do you think it is?"

She glanced at the kitchen clock, which had hung there as long as she could remember. It was almost eight. Shit, where had the day gone?

"I take it you've not made tea, then." It wasn't a question, because he already knew the answer.

"No, but you'll *never* believe what happened today."

She excitedly filled him in on the workmen's find. Dragging her husband by the arm, she showed him the hole in the wall, and the little wooden chest, and the videotapes, and lastly…

"Missing," said John. He looked at the poster for a couple of seconds, then handed it back to her, his stomach grumbling. "God, I'm starving."

She waited expectantly. "Well?"

"Well, what?"

Was he playing a trick on her? She couldn't always tell. "The girl in the poster. It's *me,* John."

"Yeah? How do you know?"

"Because she has my face."

He glanced at it again. "Kinda hard to be sure, isn't it? It's pretty faded."

An irritated noise escaped her lips. All she could do was hold the poster out to him. "John, it has my *name* written on it." She pointed to the paragraph below the photo. "Rebecca Tremayne, last seen on the twenty-sixth of December, 1984."

"Okay," he said, opening a cupboard. "Let's say it is you."

"It *is* me."

He turned to her. "Noodles fine?"

"What?" She understood the words, but they made no sense in the current context.

"For dinner. You want noodles?"

"Oh. John, the *poster.*"

"Yeah, yeah." He took the noodle packet from the cupboard and filled the kettle. "So, let's say it's you."

"Once again, it *is* me."

"Okay. So *when* were you supposedly missing?"

"I just told you. December twenty-sixth, 1984. John, that's right around the time my mum disappeared."

He paused, placing both hands on the counter, and turned to her with an expression she had grown to hate. In the early days of their marriage, he never used to look at her in that smarmy, patronising manner, like she was a silly little girl, and *he* knew better.

"Forty years, John," she said. "My mum disappeared forty years ago, just like it was forty years ago that I apparently *went missing*. Don't you find that strange? Don't you think that's an amazing coincidence?"

"Uh-huh. And you don't remember, uh, going missing?"

"Of course not! I would've mentioned it to you at some point, wouldn't I?"

"I dunno. There are a lot of things I didn't know about you until we married."

The words were a gut-punch. In their fifteen years together, John had never once raised a hand to her, but sometimes his words hurt more than physical pain ever could. "What's... what's that supposed to—"

"Forget it," he said dismissively. "You know how I get when I'm hungry." The kettle boiled, and he emptied it into a saucepan. "I'm just saying, this all seems a little... unlikely, don't you think? You would've been four years old. Wouldn't you remember *something*? Wouldn't your dad have brought it up?"

Still recovering from his earlier implication, Becky struggled to formulate a sentence. "Dad, umm, never mentioned anything," she managed to say.

"What about your sister?"

"Flora? No, nothing. Hey, what did you mean—"

"You should check with them," John interrupted. "Or — and hear me out, Becky, *please* — just drop it, you know?" He smiled at her, and placed a hand on her shoulder. "Maybe you've forgotten about it for a reason?"

Was that intended to comfort her? The idea that she was sitting on a landmine of trauma, waiting to explode...

He sighed, squeezing her shoulder in a gesture that felt more paternal than husbandly. "I'm only saying, try not to make too big a deal out if this, okay? It was a long time ago. Shit, for all we know, that poster was a joke."

"What kind of a joke?"

"I don't know. Have you seen the *Police Academy* movies? People laughed at anything in the eighties."

She didn't appreciate his dismissive nature, though her internet search for information on her potential disappearance had so far yielded no results. There were several articles about her mum, and understandably so; TV actresses didn't typically vanish without a trace. She had even found a few modern pieces about her mother, including a YouTube video titled The Top 10 Biggest Scottish Mysteries, where her mum was ranked ninth, ahead of Wee Jimmy Krankie, but behind The Loch Ness Monster.

But through all her searching, she had turned up no mentions of herself, other than references to the children her mother left behind.

Perhaps John was right.

"Okay," she said, shutting the conversation down before one of them said something they regretted.

John chuckled. "See? Not everything has to be some grand conspiracy." He went back to tending his precious fucking noodles. She caught a whiff of them, and her own stomach rumbled. When had she last eaten? Breakfast?

She placed the poster on the table and slid it away from her. "Tomorrow, I'm gonna get the tapes transferred."

"The what? The tapes?" He screwed up his face. "Are you sure that's a good idea?"

"I want to know what's on them."

"Okay. But don't blame me if it's your parents' home pornos."

"John!"

"Hey, all I'm saying is that people don't generally store videotapes in the wall."

He had a point, but Becky didn't care. She had to see. The house — bought by her parents in the late sixties —

predated home VHS recorders. She and John had taken up residence ten years ago to look after her ailing father, until they moved him to a care home when his dementia worsened. In the forty years since her mum's disappearance, no one else had lived here. The tapes *had* to belong to her parents.

She picked one up and turned it over in her hands as John ladled the steaming noodles into two bowls. She knew what he was thinking. That she was getting obsessed with something again, and that if she did — like last time — he wouldn't like the results.

Well, this wasn't about him.

What if the videos contained a clue to her mum's whereabouts? Or what if they simply offered one more chance to see her again? Either way, she wasn't going to let her husband put her off.

She slurped on some noodles and stared at the tapes.

Rumplejack.

What the hell could it mean?

She Googled '*VHS to digital transfer Edinburgh*' and scrolled through the results.

Tomorrow, she would find out.

4

The next morning, after a fitful sleep, Becky popped the videotapes in her backpack and rode the bus into town. She was ready to leave at seven-thirty, but worried the buses would be too packed with people on their way to work, and so waited an extra half-hour before leaving.

The bus was still busy, and due to the drizzling rain, the rush hour commuters had an unpleasant, damp smell about them. As the seats began to fill, Becky decided to disembark three stops early and walk the rest of the way.

Halfway down Leith Walk, the busiest street in Edinburgh's port district, she took a right, wandering through a quiet residential area. Away from the busy thoroughfare, the rainy streets took on a grim aspect. There were fewer shops here, and what remained looked like the kind of stores more likely to be fronts for money laundering schemes. She passed a second-hand furniture place and a closed-down dim sum cafe, while on the other side of the street rested the remains of a tenement ravaged by fire a few years back. The area was fenced off from the public, and signs warned of danger to life for anyone nosy enough to cross the perimeter.

She paused, gazing at the hollow shell of the ruined building.

"Huh."

Something moved on the top floor.

She wiped the rain from her eyes and saw a figure standing at the window. They looked tall, their body filling the frame, the head out of sight. Two hands, as white as bone, gripped the edges, and as the figure stooped, and the head came into view, Becky turned away. She didn't wish to be caught staring. And who would be in there, anyway? An unhoused person seeking shelter, or junkies using it as a drug den. She carried on down the street, until—

"Here we are."

She stopped outside the optimistically named *Andy's Laser Emporium* and peered through the grime-encrusted window. A tatty decal of a robot promised *'iPhones unlocked and PC repairs'* by way of a barely legible speech bubble, but the interior was dark. According to Google, the shop opened at eight-thirty, and it was currently eight-thirty-three. Should she try the door? What if it was locked?

She lit a cigarette and decided to wait. Maybe someone would go in or out, and she would find out for sure. Ten minutes and two smokes later, she muttered, "Fuck's sake." Why was it so *difficult* sometimes? Why couldn't she wander into the shop like a—

Like a what? Like a normal person?

Normal. How she loathed that word.

"You waiting fae me?"

The voice startled her. She looked up into the face of a young, bearded man in a rain-spattered blue jacket. A set of keys glinted in his hand. "Don't normally have customers first thing." He smiled disarmingly, unlocked the door to the electronics store, and held it open for her.

Inside, the place was small, and crammed from floor to ceiling with cables and adapters and assorted electrical doohickeys. Phone cases and memory cards dangled from metal pegs that jutted from the walls, creating a narrow labyrinth of consumer electronics.

"Are you Andy?" she asked.

The man walked behind the counter and dumped his jacket on the floor. "That's me," he said, as he bent awkwardly to plug in an electric heater. When he stood, he looked her dead in the eyes. "Now, what brings a lady like you tae this fine establishment?" He leaned over the glass countertop. "Need me to kill someone?"

She didn't know what to say.

"I'm kiddin' on," he laughed, his Glasgow accent shining through. Suddenly his face became deadly serious. "My killing days are over." He laughed again. "Sorry, pal, I'm still kidding on. What can I dae for you?"

On the bus, she had practiced what she would say, working through every eventuality, leaving no conversational paths untrodden. She had run the dialogue in her head, sometimes silently mouthing the words, thinking about her expressions, her tone, trying to come across as good-natured and breezy.

But the man had immediately gone rogue, and now she had to get back on script.

"Do you transfer videotapes?" she blurted, louder than she wished. She removed the tapes from her bag and held them out like an offering.

He regarded them without moving. "Aye. How long are they?"

"I don't know."

"And what's oan them?"

"I don't know that either. Is that a problem?"

"Nothing's a problem," said Andy, taking the cassettes from her. He looked them over. "Right, let's see... one-eighty, one-eighty... aye, three one-eighty tapes. You want them as files, or burned tae disc?"

"Umm, files." Then, remembering her manners, she added, "Please."

"Sick. So that'll be forty-five pounds."

"That sounds expensive."

"Then dae it yerself," he said, still smiling. "You have all the necessary equipment at home, aye?"

She didn't reply.

"Premium services come at premium prices," he explained. "Tell ya what, I'll knock a fiver off 'cos I like you, how 'bout that?"

Becky didn't like *him,* but she couldn't face trying to find another store nearby that transferred videos. It appeared to be a dying art. "Fine."

"Cash upfront."

"Naturally," she said. This prick wasn't the only one who could be sarcastic. "I need them back today."

"Nah. Winnae be ready until tomorrow. Gets busy in here on a... wait, what day is this?"

"It's Friday."

"Aye, Friday. Gets pretty busy in here on a Friday."

She glanced around the deserted store. "So I see. Is there *any* way you could have them finished by close of business tonight? It's important."

He pretended to look thoughtful. "Well, I 'spose if I shuffle a few things around, I could manage it."

"Would you? I'd appreciate that. Do you take contactless?"

"Love, this is an *electrical emporium*." He shoved the card reader towards her. "Of course we do." Before she could tap her bank card, he pulled it away. "Oh, and one more thing." He grinned in a condescending manner that reminded her of her husband. "The express service costs sixty pounds."

Becky tapped her card and paid before he could increase the cost any further.

"What time?" she asked brusquely.

"Six-thirty."

"And all three tapes will be ready?"

Andy tore off the receipt and handed it to her. "You have my word," he said, and smiled.

Somehow, she didn't believe him.

Becky stood outside the shop and closed her eyes, taking a deep breath. Okay, so it hadn't quite gone as planned, but the result was the one she wanted. The tapes would be ready in — she checked her phone — ten hours.

The workmen would be arriving soon, and if she got the bus now, she would reach her home the same time they did, and that would not do *at all*. No, it was better to let the men get to work, and try to sneak in without being spotted around lunch time.

She looked up at the burnt-out building opposite. The figure remained in the window, the hands still on the frame, almost as if the person was considering jumping. Or were they watching her?

She turned away and headed towards the main street, unusually eager to be amongst other people. As she walked, an idea came to her. She should visit her father. He was only ten minutes away by bus, and she was in a decent mental headspace today. She needed to be for visiting her dad, as his dementia had worsened in the last few years. It had nibbled away at his mind, slowly robbing him of his personality, until the man that remained was an empty husk of who he had once been.

Sometimes, secretly, she wished he would—

The bus pulled up at the stop, and she got on, watching the passers-by through rain that streaked the windows like tears. Ten minutes later, she arrived at the Springwell Care Home. The nice lady in reception greeted her fondly, and asked her to say hi to her dad. Becky promised she would, and rode the elevator up to the second floor.

He was, as usual, in his room. He never left it these days, even though he was only three doors down from the common area, where the residents could meet and talk and watch TV and play board games.

Your father enjoys his own company, a nurse had said to her once, which had made her smile.

Like father, like daughter.

On this day, he was sitting in his chair facing the wall, which was painted a sickly shade that Becky imagined was listed on colour charts as *urine stain yellow*.

"Morning, dad," she said, as cheerily as she could muster.

Wearing his pyjamas and beloved flat cap, and with a blanket across his lap, he glanced up at her, then back to the wall. A second chair sat in the corner, and Becky plonked herself on it with a tired sigh. "How are you today?"

"Oh, never better." He turned to look at her. "Are you new here? My name's Robert."

"I know, dad. It's me, Becky. Your daughter, remember?"

The old man smiled a toothless smile. "I don't have a daughter."

Rotten Tommy | 33

"Yes, you do. You have two, and one of them's sitting right here." The first dozen times they had gone through this rigmarole, it had torn Becky apart. To go unrecognised by her own father was a cruel and terrible blow for any child. But the funny thing was, she soon grew accustomed to it. Now, it was all part of the game. She no longer *expected* him to remember her. And if he did? Well, that was a bonus.

"I brought you sweets," she said, handing him a pack of Polo Mints she had picked up in the newsagent outside.

"That's kind," he said, and took them gratefully. "Have to be careful, though. These are contraband." He raised his flat cap, placed the mints on his head, and used the headwear to hide them. "Don't tell the nurses."

"It'll be our little secret."

He nodded, and resumed staring at the wall.

He looks older, Becky thought. It had been two weeks since her last visit, but he appeared to have aged a decade in that short period. His eyes were sallow and sunken, the skin around his neck sagging. It didn't help that he wasn't wearing his teeth.

"Has Flora been to visit?" she asked.

"Flora? The butter?"

"No, dad, not the butter. Your other daughter. *Flora.*"

"Oh, I don't need butter. Can't eat toast until I find my teeth, that's what the nurse said. She's mean to me." He nodded appreciatively. "But she's got a lovely arse."

"Dad!"

He laughed, his gaze never leaving the wall.

"Well, that's sweet," said Becky. "You don't remember me, but you remember your nurse's bum."

He chuckled and said nothing, while she reached into her backpack and produced a printout she had made of the 'missing' poster. She couldn't risk exposing the original to the Scottish elements, or to her father's clumsy hands.

"Dad?" She rose from the chair and handed him the poster. "Do you remember this?"

He took the printout from her with fingers that arthritis had twisted into talons. "Oh," he said, the poster trembling in his feeble grip. "*That's* my daughter."

Becky's stomach knotted. "You remember?"

"Remember? I'm not likely to forget my own flesh and blood, am I?"

"I guess not." She leaned in close and put her arm around his shoulder.

"Rebecca, we called her. After her grandmother. She's my pride and joy."

"When did she go missing?"

"Missing? No, she never went missing."

"So what about the poster? It says she was missing."

"No, that was a misunderstanding. She wasn't missing. She was on holiday."

"What do you mean? Where was she on holiday? Dad, I don't understand."

He tore his eyes from the poster and looked at her. For one heart-stopping moment, she thought he realised who she was.

"Where are my mints?" he asked. "I thought I had mints."

"They're under your hat."

"Under my hat? That's a funny place to keep them. How long have they been there?"

Becky's nails dug into her palms. "Dad, the poster. What do you mean Rebecca was on holiday? Why would there be a missing person poster?"

He spoke as if the answer was obvious. "It's simple. We thought she was missing, but she was only on holiday."

"Where?"

"Why, in Rumplejack, of course!" He looked at her with a clarity in his eyes she hadn't seen in years. "Don't you remember, Rebecca?"

The question sucked the air out of her, and she gripped his chair. "I don't remember." She tried to swallow, but her throat was parched. "Was I there with mum?"

He shook his head.

"Then who was I with?"

The smile slipped from her father's face. "You *know* we don't say his name."

Becky was frozen. Her whole body tingled.

"You smell nice," her dad said. "Are you new here?"

And he was gone again.

"No, dad. It's me, Rebecca. Don't you—"

"You've got a lovely arse."

She put a hand to her forehead and rubbed it. "Don't say that... just... don't. Please."

That was the worst part. When he forgot who she was and made lewd comments about her body. She knew he couldn't help it. She knew he didn't *mean* it. But to hear her own father talking about her in that way... it was too much.

"I have to go now," she said.

Her father nodded. He looked down at the poster. "Can I keep this?"

"Of course," she sniffed, zipping up her backpack.

"That's my daughter," he said proudly. "I wish she'd visit me."

Becky tensed. What could she say to that? "I think she'd like that too."

"Do you know her?"

"Yeah. She's very busy right now, but she asked me to tell you she loves you, and misses you, and she'll be round to visit real soon."

"That would be nice," he said contentedly. "I've not seen her for a long time." He lifted his hat, and the packet of Polo Mints rolled down his head and dropped onto his lap. "Well, would you look at that?" He glanced at Becky. "Oh! Are you new here?"

"Yeah," she said, biting her lip. "Sorry, wrong room." With that, she kissed him once on his stubbled cheek, swung her backpack over her shoulder, and left.

5

Becky arrived at *Andy's Laser Emporium* half an hour early, and spent the following thirty minutes sheltering from the rain. Andy had said six-thirty, and that was precisely when she would be there.

After visiting her father, she had returned home to trawl the internet for information on her apparent disappearance, and on the mysterious Rumplejack.

We thought she was missing, but she was only on holiday.

So Rumplejack was a place? Then why didn't it show up on any searches? She had tried various search engines — even Bing — but the closest result was 'rumblejack,' which was some kind of weapon in a video game. Dammit, was it foolish seeking sense in the ramblings of a man unable to recognise his own daughter? A man who had once possessed an active and inquisitive mind, but who now seemed only to stare at the wall and talk about lovely arses?

We don't say his name.

She glanced at the Emporium. It was the only shop on the block with the lights still on, the neon OPEN sign reflecting in the puddles. At six-twenty-nine, she stubbed her cigarette out and made her way to the door as casually as she could. Part of her expected it to be closed, but she was mistaken. The unlocked door opened soundlessly.

"Hello?" she called out, entering the store and weaving through the aisles. Something yanked her backwards, and she turned in surprise to find the hood of her raincoat snagged on a metal peg. She squirmed loose and moved warily to the counter. Andy was nowhere to be found. "Hello?" She searched in vain for a bell to ring. "Excuse me?"

There was a door behind the counter. Should she knock?

"I've come to collect my videos."

She waited. Where *was* he?

Behind her, she heard the main door open.

"Andy? Is that you?"

No reply. She peered around the corner, but there was no one there. She was all alone, so when the lights went out, Becky let out a frightened yelp.

Fuck this, she thought, and started down the aisle, aiming for the dim glow of the streetlamps. This time, there *was* someone there, waiting for her. He lurked in the shadows, blocking the aisle and obscuring the exit.

"Andy?" she asked, though she knew it wasn't.

The darkness prevented her from making out any details. He was nothing but a huge, black silhouette. *Was* it a man? Or were her eyes messing with her? She shuffled forwards, and the hulking shape moved closer.

Shit. Shit, shit, shit, shit, shit.

"I'm sorry," she said, unsure what she was apologising for. Taking a step backwards, she turned, arms outstretched, feeling her way along the aisle until her fingers brushed the roughly sanded wooden counter. Was the man following her? She couldn't take any chances, and hopped onto the counter, throwing her legs over. Her feet hit something, and it fell, crashing to the ground as she landed on the other side.

The door, the door, where was the—

It opened, and she screamed directly into the proprietor's confused face.

"What the fuck are ya doing?" Andy asked. "Customers aren't allowed back here."

"There's a man," she said breathlessly. "Back there. He's following me, and the lights went off, and—"

Andy laughed. "Oh, aye, they're on a timer. Go off at six-thirty." He hit the switch next to him, bathing the store in ugly fluorescent lighting.

"Okay, but the man…"

"What man?" Annoyance spread across Andy's bearded face, and he looked down at her feet. "You broke my mug!"

"What?"

He scooped up several pieces of shattered ceramic. "This was a collector's edition. Did ya climb over the counter?"

"Yes, because the man was following me, and it was dark, and I couldn't find—"

"Is anyone here?" Andy shouted, depositing the remains of the broken mug on the counter. "We're closed!" He turned to her, offering a smile. "See? It was your imagination. Now, what's up? I'm about tae go home."

God, he was pissing her off. There *was* someone else here. Or there had been. *Her imagination.* Jesus, he sounded like a gaslighting husband in a bad thriller.

"My tapes," she said, regaining control of her breathing. "I'm here to pick them up."

"Your what? Oh aye, I remember. There's a wee problem, I'm afraid."

Of course there was.

She bit her tongue. "Are they ready or not? I paid extra."

"Nah, no' ready. One of them is. But there were technical difficulties."

"Technical difficulties?"

"Aye. With the tapes, mind, no' with my equipment. I had to, uh, re-digitise the isolation vectors."

Becky had spent the previous night reading up on how to transfer videotapes to digital, and she was fairly certain that Andy's explanation was a load of bollocks.

"So you only managed one?"

"That's right. It's through the back. Wait here, I'll get it."

The door slammed closed, and he was gone again. What if the other man was still there? Well, he would have to come get her, because she was not moving a fucking inch from behind the counter.

The door opened, red light spilling out, and Andy re-emerged clutching something in his hand. "Here you go," he said, handing her a thumb drive and the cassette. "Want me to throw the tape away for you?"

"No thanks, I'll keep it."

"Suit yourself."

She waited for him to say something else, and they stood in awkward silence. "What about the other tapes? When will they be ready?"

"Tomorrow."

"What time?"

"Well, it's Saturday, so I dinnae open until ten."

"And they'll be ready for ten? Both of them?"

"Scout's honour," he grinned. "I'll dae them overnight, especially for you."

"Really?"

"Come on... don't you trust me?"

She didn't. "Ten o'clock, then. They'd better be ready."

What the hell did she mean by *that?* Was that a threat? Luckily, he ignored her, and the feeling of disappointment gave way to excitement. She stuffed the video and the thumb drive in her backpack and left without saying goodbye, forgetting all about the strange man she had encountered in the darkness.

～

Andy watched the woman leave.

She was daft as a brush. He wondered if he could charge her extra for breaking his mug? He doubted she'd complain. All she wanted was those tapes transferred, and no wonder. Did she know what she had there? An absolute goldmine!

Dammit, if he'd acted faster, he could have had all three ready like he'd promised. But he'd spent most of the day on the Baldur's Gate forums, and now he'd have to stay late. Potentially six *hours* late. But it would all be worth it. If the remaining tapes contained similar footage... fuck, he couldn't wait to tell Serge about it. Actually...

He checked the time. Serge would be finished work. Andy unlocked his phone and called Serge as he retreated to the back room. His lair, as he liked to describe it.

"Here, Serge, ya knob," he said, as the man answered. Andy smiled, and turned his eyes to the monitor, on which played the footage from the first of the woman's tapes. "You're not gonna *believe* what I've found. We've just hit the fucking jackpot, ya cunt. The fucking *jackpot.*"

6

It had been a long day for Becky.

The rain never let up, and her sodden shoes squelched repulsively with each step. John had texted to say he'd be home late, and though she normally didn't mind, for once in her life she craved company. Really, what she wanted was someone to watch the video with her. For some inexplicable reason, she was afraid to. What if it was blank? Or just episodes of *Family Fortunes* and *Blind Date?* The chances of the tapes containing some magical clue as to her mother's whereabouts were practically non-existent. And yet, they *had* been hidden in the wall, which was not normal behaviour, even in *her* family.

She barely remembered her mum. Fleeting glimpses were all she had left, fragments of shattered memories rattling around in her head. She had been four years old when her mother vanished. All she recalled from back then was the image of her dad sitting in his chair, sobbing, while the baby cried for attention upstairs.

Forty years ago.

No wonder her memory was hazy. One thing she was

certain of was that she had never heard the word Rumplejack before. But then, twenty-four hours earlier, she would have sworn she had never gone missing as a child, and now even *that* was up for debate.

"Fuck," she said. She needed someone to talk to. Someone understanding, a friend who could listen and offer advice. Unfortunately, she couldn't think of anyone, so she decided to visit her sister Flora instead.

They could watch the video together. She wondered if Flora remembered something, a clue that would help make sense of things. Perhaps Rumplejack was a resort for children, and *Flora* had been the one to holiday there?

By the time she reached her sister's street, the rain had halted, and a mocking sliver of sunlight bathed the streets in a warm orange glow. Flora lived in a second floor flat, and Becky shielded her eyes from the sun and peered up at the windows. The curtains were drawn. She rang the buzzer and waited, thinking she should have texted to let her sister know she—

Bzzzzzz

The door jolted Becky from her thoughts. She pushed it open and entered the stairwell. Typical Flora, not checking to see who had rung the bell. A handwritten note was taped to the wall, with the words KEEP THE DOOR LOCKED NIGHT AND DAY written on it. "Doesn't matter," said Becky, as she started up the stairs. "Flora will let *anyone* in."

On the second floor, she paused to catch her breath. Flora's door was closed, an unwelcoming gesture that was on-brand for her sister. Still, she was here now, and may as well try to make the best of it. Surely even her legendarily selfish sibling would be interested in seeing a video that had been secreted within the walls of their childhood home?

Becky placed her hand on the door and opened it,

surprised to find Flora waiting on the other side. The woman had her back to the door, and she wore nothing but a thong and thigh-high stockings.

"Hello, lover," cooed Flora, running her hands down her sides. She bent over, revealing the thin strip of material between her bum cheeks.

Growing up with an exhibitionist sister, it was nothing Becky hadn't seen before.

"Uh, were you expecting someone else?"

Flora's posture slumped. Still bent over, she peered at Becky through her own spread legs, her hair brushing across the floor. "Oh, it's you."

"Charming. You think you could stand up? I'd rather not talk to your arsehole."

Flora did. She turned to Becky and crossed her arms. "Are you still here? In case you hadn't noticed, I've got a date coming round."

"A date?"

"Well, a shag. But I'm expecting him soon, so scurry along." She waved her hands as if shooing Becky away.

"I'll just be a second. Do you want to, uh, put some clothes on?"

"No."

"Okay. Well, if we went inside, we—"

"I already told you, I'm busy. You can't stay."

Fucking Flora. She's such a—

No, don't say it.

It was a terrible word to call another woman. Flora wasn't a bitch.

She was a *cunt*.

"Becky!" shouted Flora. "Would you stop grinning and tell me what this is about before my pussy dries up completely?"

Rotten Tommy | 45

Becky was losing her. She had to act quickly. "Remember when mom disappeared?"

"No, I was a baby."

"Oh, yeah. Well, did dad ever mention me going missing?"

"No. Anything else?"

"Ummm..." The conversation was moving too fast. Flora knew what she was doing.

Concentrate, dammit!

"What about Rumplejack?"

"I don't know what that means. Are we done?"

"No!" she shouted.

Flora raised an eyebrow and took a step closer, holding the edge of the door, ready to close it.

"I found videotapes," blurted Becky. "Mum and dad's secret videotapes. I've had one transferred. Want to watch it with me?"

Flora chuckled. "Oh sweet, innocent Becky. Take my advice. Do *not* watch those tapes."

"Why not? What do you know?"

"All I know is that when a mummy and a daddy love each other very much, they sometimes make their own—"

"Okay, fine, I get it," said Becky, as Flora laughed at her. "That's exactly what John said. You two are as bad as each other."

"Great minds," smiled Flora, as she started to close the door.

"Yeah, sure. Maybe you two should have married," Becky called out, as Flora closed the door on her. "I hope your sex is *rubbish!*" she bellowed, the echo reverberating off the stairwell's bare, marble-effect walls. She ran her hands through her hair, then started down the stairs. God, it was as if her sister possessed some arcane knowledge about how best to piss her off.

The rain was on again, and she decided to take the bus home.

We thought she was missing, but she was only on holiday.

Her father's words rang in her ears.

We don't say his name.

Whose name? She had no idea. And as she strode through the gloomy evening drizzle, she passed a group of children huddled together. Keeping her head down, she walked by. Children made her uncomfortable. They were too unpredictable. In her periphery, she saw they were holding hands and chanting a rhyme.

"Keep the door locked night and day,
So Tommy can't come out to play."

The words were familiar to her, but she couldn't place them.

"Keep the door locked night and day,
So Tommy can't come out to play."

Over and over they chanted, the words as meaningless as any children's song.

"Keep the door locked night and day,
So Tommy can't come out to play."

But something about it... something...

"And if you knock on the big wooden door..."

The children laughed.

"Tommy will..." whispered Becky.

Tommy will *what*? Why did those two words pop into her head? She turned to the children, but they were gone.

"And if you knock on the big wooden door," repeated Becky. "Tommy will..."

She knew the rest of the words. She was convinced of it.

They were in her head somewhere, sealed in a vault, unable to be accessed.

She typed the lyrics into her phone so she wouldn't forget them.

"Tommy," she whispered, and resumed walking, suddenly eager to be home and safe and out of the rain. As she did, the words of her father drifted through her mind like smoke.

We don't say his name.
You know we don't say his name.

7
―――

WITH JOHN STAYING LATE AT THE BANK, AND THE BUILDERS away until work resumed on Monday, the house was quiet.

It was sheer bliss.

The refrigerator hummed in the next room, and outside, a dog barked somewhere down the street, but otherwise, all was still. Becky poured herself a glass of lemonade, switched off the lights, and settled herself on the couch. With anticipation building, she inserted the thumb drive into her laptop and transferred the file onto her computer.

She couldn't believe Flora had no interest in watching it. Then again, the woman had always lacked curiosity, even when they were children. What Flora *had* been blessed with was confidence. Whereas Becky grew up painfully shy and anxious, Flora strode through life unconcerned with what people thought, potential suitors begging for a chance to woo her.

Her sister had always been popular with the boys. Despite being younger than Becky, she lost her virginity first, to a Spanish exchange student several years her senior. And by the time Becky started dating John, her future husband and first real boyfriend, Flora had already been divorced. In some ways, Becky envied her sister. She tried not to, but it was difficult when the woman excelled at everything she was hopeless at.

"I got mum's confidence and beauty," Flora had said one time. *"And you got dad's autism."*

It had been said in jest, but Flora was proven correct a few years later, when Becky received her autism diagnosis. It had come as no surprise to either woman. John, on the other hand...

The file finished transferring, and Becky double-clicked to open it in VLC Player.

"Here we go," she whispered.

A hiss of static assaulted the screen, before a picture crackled into view, thick tracking lines scarring the image. It was dark. It was... outer space? A ship roared into view from the top of the screen.

Becky's heart sank. My god, had she just paid sixty pounds for a copy of *Star Wars* in VHS Shit-o-Vision? The DVD box set was upstairs in John's entertainment room! At least Flora wasn't here to witness her embarrassment. The picture shook, tinny sound spluttering from the speakers, and then the image changed.

A black screen, with numbers running across the top. Becky knew it was a time-code. She had a collection of her mum's old tapes, videos of her TV work before they were broadcast, and they usually had a time-code stamp on them.

The numbers on this tape were hard to read, the black background a dull, washed-out grey, but seconds later the Golden Thistle logo appeared. It was more yellow than the gold Becky remembered from her childhood.

Urine stain yellow.

Anticipation flooded her mind, along with relief that

John and Flora's 'home porno' theory had proven incorrect. A vintage synthesiser burbled in the background, and the screen cut to a blurred view of an idyllic coastal town.

Rumplejack, read the onscreen title card in a whimsical, almost medieval font. The synth music droned on, and a voice joined in. It sounded like a little girl singing.

"Let's go back,
To Rumplejack,
We've been away too long."

The poor audio quality caused the voice to raise and lower in pitch, distorting the melody.

"Your friends await,
So don't be late,
To help them sing this song."

The image changed to a shot of a lighthouse, the sky behind it dreich and miserable. A figure — it looked like a woman, though it was hard to tell — entered the frame.

"Rumplejack, oh Rumplejack," warbled the lone, ethereal voice. *"You're never far away. Rumplejack, oh Rumplejack, I wish that I could stay."*

Things were beginning to make sense. Rumplejack was the name of a TV show, presumably one starring her mum. Becky had never been on *holiday* there. Her poor father had muddled his memories, that was all.

No, that couldn't be the case. She knew her mum's filmography inside and out, and there was no mention of Rumplejack anywhere. Why did the title not show up on the internet? Nothing remained buried there. Even the most obscure television series had a fan site or a Wiki article, and surely *someone* who worked on Rumplejack must have posted about it?

The song ended, and the camera glided alongside the woman as she limped towards the lighthouse. Ambient noise filled the audio track, which pulsated from the speakers, rising in volume then dropping to nothing, almost as if it was breathing.

The lighthouse stood atop a rocky outcrop. Waves crashed against the sides as the wind howled mournfully against the round, greying walls. Becky smiled. She adored lighthouses. As a child, she had been obsessed by them.

The woman shouted, snapping Becky's attention back to the show. The dialogue was muffled, almost inaudible, but it sounded like she was calling for—

"Sausage King? Are you there?"

Becky chuckled. Sausage King? Children's television was so weird. She supposed the shows she had watched as a child had been equally bizarre.

The woman made her way up the lighthouse, navigating the spiral staircase with practiced slowness. Becky assumed she was watching an early rough cut, as there was no chance an episode with pacing this glacial would ever make it to broadcast.

She sat closer. "Wait a minute."

The screen had glitched. Using the laptop trackpad, she dragged the slider back a few seconds, and there it was again. As fast as a blink, and inserted into a rather tedious shot of the woman dragging her gammy leg up the stairs, were a couple of frames — mere fractions of a second — of darkness. No, not darkness...

Becky rewound, pausing the image and using the E key to move frame by frame until she isolated the moment.

She squinted at the screen. "What the hell am I looking at?"

Raising the brightness on her laptop didn't help. She thought she made out a silhouette; round shoulders, a bulbous head... but it was too dark to be certain.

"Bad editing, that's all."

She hit the space bar to resume playing, and the woman continued her ascent up the lighthouse stairs. The synth music gurgled to nothingness, the soundtrack becoming an eerie bed of squawking gulls. Becky imagined children all across Scotland switching channels to *Puddle Lane* or *The Family Ness* in sheer boredom. She understood why *Rumplejack* had never been broadcast. Still, was it shite enough to hide inside a wall for forty years? That seemed like an overreaction.

The mystery woman opened a hatch and clambered up a wooden ladder to the lighthouse gallery. She inspected the lens, then hauled a chair out onto the wide catwalk that circled the lantern room, the metal legs screeching across the floor. Struggling to keep her dress under control from the ferocious winds, the woman sat, and the camera cut to a closeup.

"Oh," said Becky.

The woman was severely burnt. She had no hair — not that Becky could see on the poor quality recording, anyway — and her head was a mass of pink and white scar tissue. Her nose was skull-like, her teeth showing through a charred, lipless grimace. She was, to put it mildly, an unusual sight for a children's TV show.

Tracking lines assailed the screen, splitting the image in two, the top half an inch further to the left than the bottom half.

"Ah, good old VHS."

Becky maintained some fondness for the format — until the advent of the internet, it had been the only conduit to her absent mother — but it was useless as a long-term storage device.

"Are you happy?"

The voice came from out of nowhere. For one mad second, Becky thought someone was talking to *her*. Then the image shifted to a mangy hand puppet. The fawn fur, black ears, and flappy pink tongue suggested it was meant to be a pug dog. The puppet tilted his head, and Becky tried to picture the human hand inside him, operating the mouth in gloriously lo-fi fashion.

"Are you happy?" the puppet repeated, in a voice that sounded like the old English actor James Mason had inhaled helium.

The show cut back to the woman, who held a string of sausages in her hand.

"Well, *they* weren't there a second ago," said Becky, a wry grin on her face.

"All hail The Sausage King," the woman said, letting the sausages dangle over the hand puppet's eager, open mouth. She released them, and they appeared to fall into the waiting gullet. It was a clever special effect, Becky had to admit. There must have been a hole in the puppet's mouth, black fabric doubtlessly hiding the fleshy and all-too-human digits within. She wondered if the woman was the one operating him.

Offscreen, the pug chewed noisily on the sausages, as the woman watched the sun rising over the choppy waters. A warm sensation spread throughout Becky, as if she felt nostalgic for a place she had never visited.

"Thank you for the sausages," said the pug.

The Sausage King, Becky corrected herself, and giggled. *Show him some respect.*

"Now, please tell me. Are you happy?"

The woman gazed at the horizon. *"I am. I'm happy."*

"And that's the woof," said The Sausage King.

"Don't you mean the truth?"

"But that's what I said... and that's the woof!"

"Oh boy," said Becky. With that dreadful wordplay, *Rumplejack,* for the first time since the opening theme song, actually felt like what it was supposed to be; bad children's television.

Could there possibly be three more hours of this? Or even another *nine?* If so, she didn't mind. The show possessed an off-kilter quality that appealed to her sensibilities, like David Lynch directing an episode of *Sesame Street.*

"Sure thing, Sausage King," the woman said. *"And that's the woof."*

"That's the woof," whispered Becky, before the screen went black. When the image reappeared a few seconds later, it depicted a horse, standing on his hind legs, and dressed as a cowboy. *Very* obviously a man in an ill-fitting costume, he kept one hoof pressed against the wall for balance, scraping the brickwork as he lounged in his stetson, waistcoat, and brown leather chaps.

Becky chuckled. "What now?"

"Howdy folks," said the cowboy. *"My name's Stick'emup, and I'm sheriff round these parts."* He appeared to be addressing the audience. *"You want a tour of my police station?"* He pointed a hoof at the furniture. *"This here is where I book the bad guys into jail."* The sheriff's voice was more conventional than The Sausage King's. In fact, he sounded a lot like a Wild West version of Goofy, and Becky pondered whether the show had been removed for legal reasons, such as a Disney copyright infringement lawsuit.

"You wanna see my jail?" asked Stick'emup, and the camera followed the horse, getting so close that the lens bumped into his stetson, knocking it askew. Inside, the cowboy gestured at the cells. Becky listened carefully. She swore she heard someone crying.

"I got all the bad guys in here. Except that Sausage King." Stick'emup pounded his hooves together. *"But I'll get him one day!"*

"What about Tommy?" asked an offscreen voice, and nothing happened for so long that Becky had to check to ensure the screen hadn't frozen. *"What about Tommy? What about Tommy?"*

A chorus of voices joined in; men, women, and children, their feet stamping, hands clapping.

"What about Tommy, what about Tommy, what about Tommy?" they sang, as two bloodstained hands reached into frame and grabbed Stick'emup by his plush neck, yanking him towards the jail cell bars. A woman's face appeared, bruised and battered, as she clung onto the cowboy with arms that vibrated with crazed fury.

"What about Tommy?" she screamed, her fingers digging into his neck. *"What about Tommy, you cunt? Huh? You fucking piece of shit cunt motherfu—"*

The screen cut out.

Becky sat in silence. She felt something wet on her thighs, and realised she had spilt her lemonade. The glass in her hand shook so violently that what little liquid remained sloshed from side-to-side like the waves that crashed eternally against Rumplejack lighthouse...

"No," she said, as she rubbed at her eyes the way she always did when she was stressed.

What about Tommy, you cunt? Huh? You fucking piece of shit cunt motherfu—

It wasn't possible.

What the fuck.

She felt sick.

What the fuck, what the fuck, what the fuck fuck fuck.

She scrolled back, finding a clear shot of the woman, and paused on her bloodied, screaming face.

What about Tommy, you cunt? Huh? You fucking piece of shit cunt motherfu—

"Good god," whispered Becky.

There was no doubt about it.

The woman on the screen...

It was her mother.

8

In the red-lit back room of *Andy's Laser Emporium*, Andy Malcolm reclined in his gaming chair, an open beer on the table next to the computer monitor. He was watching the recording of the second tape as the third transferred, and this one was a doozy.

Rumplejack.

What the giddy fuck *was* this show? He didn't know, but it was gonna make him and Serge famous. The pair ran a YouTube channel — *Land of the Lost Media* — in which they discussed and dissected TV shows and films that were considered missing. From early episodes of *Doctor Who* and *The Quatermass Experiment* to the absent director's cut of *Event Horizon* and the deleted piranha bait sequence from *Cannibal Holocaust,* Andy and Serge produced hours of content in their quest to unearth this hidden material. There was something about the search that made the two lads from Glasgow feel like time travelling archaeologists. The only problem was, they never actually found any of the footage they were looking for.

But now *Rumplejack* had fallen into Andy's sweaty lap.

How about that for a scoop? A piece of lost media *so* lost that no one knew it existed! Andy considered himself a connoisseur of eighties pop culture, in particular kids TV shows. When transferring the woman's tape, he had watched, fascinated, as the bizarre and twisted drama unfolded. It was obvious why the show was never broadcast; it was fucking bananas. One five-minute sequence in episode one was a static shot of an empty nightclub. And if the show never quite reached the high of the mad bitch trying to strangle the fucker in the horse costume through the cell bars, it often came close. As for the subliminal edits... well, those alone would produce enough content for an episode of *Land of the Lost Media*.

Andy scrolled through the timeline, searching for one of those moments where the screen briefly darkened. He would need to jot down the times, which was easy thanks to the timecode in the top corner. Once isolated, he would get Serge to fuck around with them in Photoshop. He found one, and freeze-framed the image.

Funny.

The big, hunched man was completely missing. He kept scrolling, as far as the opening lighthouse walk, and waited for the subliminal edit to appear, afraid to blink in case he missed it.

"Gotcha," he grinned, hitting pause and taking a swig of beer. When he looked at the screen, the figure was absent again. Had he imagined it? In his excitement at stumbling across an unaired, previously unseen TV series, had he spotted something that wasn't there? The screen displayed a grey wall, with what looked like — if he screwed up his eyes *real* hard — a typewriter on a desk at the very bottom of the frame.

"Nah, man. There was some cunt sitting there." He

would swear on his nan's grave, and the old boot wasn't even dead yet.

He closed the app and reverted his gaze to the tape being transferred, which appeared to be a home movie. Ah, he wasn't interested in that. All he could do was hope that the third tape contained more footage. The internet was going to lose its collective mind over this.

He took one more look at the screen — a middle-aged man in a paper party hat reclined in a chair, waving at the camera — and decided to take a piss. He didn't have a toilet in the shop, but there was a narrow alley between the buildings he used in emergencies.

Unlocking the side door, Andy stepped out into the freezing drizzle. Christ, did it ever stop raining? He unzipped his fly, pulled out his cock, and pissed against the neighbouring shop's wall. Why not? The owners were cunts. He glanced to his right to make sure no one on the street could see him, then, instinctively, to the dead end on his left.

Someone was there.

A tall figure, cloaked in shadows.

"Oi, who's that?" shouted Andy, keeping his eyes on the man, steam rising from where his urine arced against the wall. There *was* someone there... wasn't there? It was hard to tell. The streetlamps stretched only partially down the alleyway, and the moon was lost behind a battalion of thick storm clouds.

The shadowy figure took a step closer. Fuck, he was huge, towering over Andy, who already stood a healthy six-three in his socks.

"You watching me piss, ya pervy wanker?" shouted Andy. "Fuck off!"

Andy was afraid of no man, having grown up in Glasgow's infamous Possilpark during the eighties. Still, this fucker was massive.

The big man moved closer, stepping partly into the glow of the streetlamp. Light reflected off something metal in the man's hand. A knife? No, not a knife. Andy squinted through the rain.

It was a meat tenderiser.

Andy's stream of piss dried up. "Awright, ya big goth. Calm doon. I've no' got any money on me." Sure, Andy could handle himself, but it was never a good idea to start a fight with a mad bastard who was armed. "Listen, you'd be better off robbin' some cunt fae Stockbridge or Morningside. Or hang around they new student flats. Naebody here has any money."

The man's face remained drenched in shadow. He was utterly still.

Andy zipped up his fly and backed away. "We alright then, pal? We good? Seriously, try Stockbridge. I guarantee they posh cunts won't put up a fight."

Then the man walked fully into the light, and the last of Andy's piss dribbled down his leg.

"Jesus," he said, stumbling backwards, grasping for the door handle as the man came for him.

That's no man. Look at his face!

Andy shoved his way inside. The meat tenderiser cracked against his shoulder blade, and he screamed, slamming the door behind him. It bounced harmlessly off the big man, who thrust it open with such ferocity that the whole door tore from its hinges. He had to stoop to enter, and Andy caught another glimpse of that impossible, maddening face.

"Who are you?"

The man stalked towards him. Blood dripped from the

mallet's shallow spikes, leaving a trail throughout the darkened backroom.

"Leave me alone. Leave me the fuck alone!"

Andy bumped into the wall. The door to the shop was next to him, and he threw it open, reaching below the register, groping for—

His baseball bat.

He had only used it once before, when some jakies had tried to nick his product. Now, it was going to have to save his life. He raced back into the computer room, and, with a mighty yell, went on the offensive. He clubbed the bat across the man's chest. It was like hitting a sledgehammer against concrete, the vibrations tingling through Andy's limbs. He tried again, aiming higher. The wooden club thudded against the man's head, severely denting it.

"Oh fuck," said Andy, as the bat slipped from his loose grasp.

The man was unmoved by the violence. He reached his free hand up to his head, to the concave area where the bat had struck, and pressed his fingers into the pale, doughy softness, stretching it out like he was made of clay. When he let go, four finger holes remained in the distended flesh.

"What the fuck are you?" groaned Andy.

The man answered by shoving him backwards. Andy's head struck the wall, and he slid to the ground, his vision swooning. The big man knelt before him, his black leather smock creasing. He grabbed Andy by his belt and dragged him closer.

"Please," was all Andy could utter.

The man hovered above him, then slammed the tenderiser down on Andy's chest. Ribs shattered, the noise deafening in the quiet room, and when the man pulled the tenderiser away, it snagged on Andy's flesh, gashing him open. Again and again the man smacked the blunt implement against him, snapping and crushing his bones. He thought he might pass out, and then the tenderiser swept through the air and landed on his hand, obliterating it. The hammer hit the floor, blood spurting wildly from the ruined appendage.

"Kill me!" he spluttered.

The man didn't. He resumed pounding the tenderiser against Andy's chest and stomach. Blood pooled around him as the weapon tore his skin to shreds, and when the man raised it for the final time, strings of wet, blood-slicked intestines hung from the handle like carcasses in a butcher shop window.

The pale man reached inside Andy, looping the revolting tubes around his wrist and yanking his guts loose. Andy's brain flooded with chemicals, and all he could do was watch as the giant carelessly disembowelled him. Somehow, it was the smell that was the worst, the smell of his own organs, of his own blood, of his own shit. The man tossed the useless viscera aside, the innards splatting over the computer desk and slithering to the floor in sloppy, obscene coils.

As Andy drew his last breaths, and the man raised the now-crimson hammer high above his unprotected face, a single line from that fucking show ran through his head.

What about Tommy, you cunt? What about Tommy, you cunt? What about Tommy, you cunt? What about—

Then the meat tenderiser split his skull like an egg, and Andy Malcolm thought no more.

9

"That's your mother?" asked John. "Are you sure?"

"Of course I'm sure," said Becky. "I know my own mum."

"Okay, don't bite my head off. It's been a while since you saw her, that's all I mean."

Seated around the kitchen table, John chewed on microwave curry as they watched the video. He had been late home from work again, and she had corralled him straight into the kitchen, refusing his requests for a shower first. Could he not understand how important this was to her?

"And you said this was a kids' show?" he asked, spooning tikka masala into his mouth.

"I think so. It looks like it, kinda. There are puppets and songs, but everything feels... off."

"Yeah. I can't imagine Andi Peters dropping the 'C' word in the BBC broom cupboard." He pointed at the frozen image of Becky's mum on the laptop. "She's good, though. Your mum's not normally so... gritty."

The chair creaked beneath Becky as she adjusted

herself, trying to decide how best to proceed. "John... what if she's not acting?"

"What?"

"I mean, *look* at her. What if this is, y'know, real?"

Her husband was silent. The familiar expression darkened his features. "Becky, what are you saying? It's a TV show. A weird one, for sure, but it's not *real*. Your mum's acting. That's what actresses *do*."

"No, you don't understand. I've seen her so often, I've watched every video I have of her, hundreds of times. And this," she said, pointing at the screen, "is different. She looks really scared."

"She's strangling a man in a horse costume."

"Yeah, but—"

"The horse is dressed as a cowboy."

She sighed, and he placed a comforting hand on hers.

"Becky, listen to me."

"I am."

"Then look me in the eyes."

Christ, how many times did she have to tell him she hated doing that? He took her chin and raised her head, and she stared at the bridge of his nose.

"What else have you done today?" he asked. "Did you work on your script?"

"Um, no, but I've been researching this show. John, it's crazy, there's no record of—"

"Aren't you *supposed* to be working on a script?" He asked as if they both didn't know the answer.

"Yes."

"And when's the deadline?"

"Soon."

He smiled. "So is this *really* a productive use of your time? You're chasing shadows. Your mum's gone, okay? She's been gone for a long time, and this video isn't going to change anything. I don't want to see you disappear down one of your rabbit-holes again. You know how you get with things like this. You get obsessed, and it's not healthy for us."

"Us?"

"For you," he corrected, his smile more pained than before. "It's *you* I'm worried about." He closed the laptop. "Come on, go to bed. You're always up so late, it might do you good to get a decent night's sleep instead of watching some old TV show so bad that even the people who *made* it never released it."

The people who made it.

Shit, why hadn't she thought of that before? The filmmakers!

"You're right," she said, trying to mask her excitement. "I think I'll go to bed and work on my script."

"That's my girl." Brightening, he squeezed her hand, finally allowing her to look away. "Promise you're not gonna watch that video another hundred times?"

She ignored the question. "You staying up?"

"Yeah. It's Friday night, y'know. Might have a beer and put on a movie."

"You're a wildman," she said, and though he replied, Becky didn't hear him, because she was already halfway up the stairs with the laptop tucked under her arm.

The damn filmmakers! Their names were listed in the end credits. The show was forty years old, so surely *some* of the cast and crew were still alive. She could find them on Facebook and enquire about *Rumplejack*. Someone might be willing to talk about it, and hopefully shed some light on the production.

And maybe, just maybe... they would have some information on her mother.

She retrieved her pyjamas from the wardrobe at the foot of the bed, slipped into them, and snuggled under the duvet, keeping the door ajar in case she heard John coming up the stairs. With her script open and ready as a decoy, she opened the video file and skipped straight to the closing credits, which appeared an astonishing fifty-four minutes into the episode. That was unheard of for eighties children's TV, where episodes generally ranged from five to twenty minutes.

Rumplejack's credits rolled over a freeze-frame of the lighthouse, with the lonesome sound of squawking gulls replacing any accompanying music. She tried to read the names as they scrolled, but they were so fast, and the picture quality was so shoddy, that she struggled to find any legible ones. Even when she hit pause, the video-generated titles overlapped, turning into hieroglyphics.

"Jacob..." she whispered, "Moretti? Morelli? Horelli?"

Christ, maybe it wasn't Jacob. Jason? Dammit, she had a spreadsheet ready and waiting to be filled in, and she couldn't make out a single name. She pressed play, letting the sound of distant seabirds lull her mind. This time, though, she heard another noise. Subdued singing, low in the audio mix. A child's voice. Could she raise the volume, or would that alert John? There was no sound from downstairs, which suggested he was wearing his expensive cordless headphones.

Becky took the chance. She tapped the volume button on the keyboard. Oddly, it only raised the squawks of the gulls, drowning the soft singing out completely. She lowered the volume, bringing the voice back to the forefront.

"That shouldn't be possible," she said, and paused the video.

The singing continued uninterrupted.

She closed the laptop, but nothing silenced the voice.

Becky's throat was dry. She tried to speak, but no words came out, and when she glanced over at the wardrobe, she realised…

The singing was coming from inside.

10

Becky's hands trembled as she laid the laptop on John's side of the bed.

She could make the words out perfectly now.

"Keep the door locked night and day, so Tommy can't come out to play," crooned the child's sickly voice, over and over like a scratched record.

"Who's there?"

The maddening rhyme continued.

"John?" she called out. *"John!"*

Damn his stupid headphones!

What should she do? It wasn't as if she could ignore it and fall asleep. She had to investigate.

Becky slipped out from under the covers, her bare feet finding the reassuring comfort of the hardwood floor.

"Keep the door locked night and day, so Tommy can't come out to play."

She looked around for a weapon, but other than a dimmable lamp, the bedside table offered only a can of deodorant, a contact lens case, a paperback novel, and her hairbrush. Her laptop was the only item to hand that could cause damage, but laptops were expensive. Her gaze settled on John's golf clubs in the far corner of the room. She never liked having them in the house, and hated the way the wheeled bag trailed grass and mud through the hallway, but at least now they might prove useful. She crawled across the bed, scurrying past the wardrobe, and lifted one free.

After calling her husband's name one more time, she rested the golf club on her shoulder and took a tentative step closer to the old oak wardrobe, reaching for the handle. The metal knob was icy to the touch. Gripping it in fragile fingers, Becky took a breath and yanked the door open.

At once, the singing stopped. A rail of clothes hung before her, some items sealed in plastic covers that reminded her of body bags hanging in cold storage. The garments swayed as if recently disturbed.

Call for John again.

No, he wouldn't believe her. Keeping her distance, she used the golf club to spread the clothes apart. The metal scraped along the back of the wardrobe. There was nobody there.

"*Nobody,*" she whispered, stepping back and closing the door, her eyes catching movement by the curtains, a deathly pale hand reaching from the other side and drawing the curtain back, revealing—

"*Fuck!*" she screamed, racing forwards and battering the curtain with the golf club. She brought the weapon down hard, ripping the curtain from the rail and smashing the window. Shards of glass rained down on the garden path outside, the loose curtain falling and draping itself around her like a death shroud. She fought to free herself, tumbling backwards, and then hands were on her, tight hands pinning her down.

"Get off me!" she screamed, kicking out and making good contact.

"Oof!" cried John, as he pulled the heavy fabric off her. "What the fuck are you doing?"

"There's someone in here," she said, scrambling to her feet.

"You smashed the fucking window!"

"He was behind the curtains!"

"Who?"

She moved towards the window, and John pushed her onto the bed. Shocked, she looked up at him.

"There's glass everywhere," he spat angrily. "Watch your feet." He stared out the window, tiny shards crunching beneath the soles of his slippers.

"There was a person singing, I swear, and when... when I..."

John kicked the glass against the sideboard, shaking his head. He turned to her, his face crimson with fury.

"They were in there," she said, pointing to the wardrobe.

"In the fucking *wardrobe?*" He spoke like every word was an effort.

Becky nodded.

"So why'd you smash the window?"

Before she could answer, he stalked round the bed and grabbed her laptop. She reached for it, but he was too fast. He opened the laptop, displaying the end credits of Rumplejack. "I thought we agreed you weren't going to watch this again?"

She couldn't respond. Her words were all dried up.

"See, I told you this would happen. I told you not to watch, not to get obsessed like you always do whenever some new idiotic notion catches your eye. What good's gonna come of this? What do you hope to find? Can't you just be..."

"What?" she croaked. "Be normal?"

"Yes! You never used to be like this. Not until you became autistic."

"I've *always* been autistic," she said, still lying on the bed where he had shoved her. She doubted she could stand even if she wanted to. "It never bothered you until it had a name."

"No, you've gotten worse. This whole 'unmasking' thing you're trying, it needs to stop. It's..."

"It's what?"

"It's embarrassing, that's what it is. What grown woman sleeps with a cuddly toy in her bed, or can't go into a restaurant unless someone goes in first, or knows all the words to *Monty Python's Holy* fucking *Grail?* You're in your forties, for crying out loud. Grow up!" He seemed to realise he'd said too much, and sighed like a pantomime dame. "Enough with the videos, okay? And don't bother Flora with them either, she doesn't—"

"When did you talk to my sister?"

He looked surprised. "Huh? She called me. *Texted* me, said you'd been, uh, harassing her."

"Do you often text each other?"

"What? I think you're missing the point here." He closed the laptop and tucked it under his arm. "Okay, no more computer time for you tonight. Go to bed, and get some sleep."

"*Computer time?* John, give me my laptop back."

"No. If you can't be trusted, I'm going to have to confiscate it."

She glared at him. "It's mine. *Give it back.*"

He regarded her with a look of contempt. "You can get it in the morning."

"How fucking dare you?" Her fists clenched, and despite the confusion and shame, she managed to stand. "I'm your *wife,* you prick. Not a child."

"Then stop acting like one, and I won't have to punish you." He turned away, stomping down the hallway.

"You fucker," said Becky, giving chase. "Punish me? *Punish* me?" She caught up to him and pounded her fists against his broad back. "Give me my laptop back!"

Shit.

She felt it coming on. A full-blown meltdown. Though prone to them as a child and teenager, it had been years since her last one. As an adult, she had learnt to extricate herself from stressful situations that brought them on. But she was too far gone now, and though she knew she should stop, that she was only going to prove John right — at least in his own mind — she couldn't. Her whole body shook, her mind clouding over.

It was unavoidable.

"Give me it back!" she screamed, sobbing now, striking him with her fists. "It's mine!"

"Listen to yourself!" he roared back. "You're a grown woman throwing a fucking tantrum!" She moved closer, and he shoved her backwards. Becky stumbled over her own feet and landed on her arse. Without waiting to see if she was okay, John walked away.

"You fucker!" She rose unsteadily, heart pounding, and followed him down the stairs. She found him in the living room, sitting on the settee while *Would I Lie To You?* played on the telly. "Where is it? Where's my laptop?"

He ignored her, placing the headphones on his head and crossing his arms like the smug bastard he was. Becky grabbed his mug of beer and tossed the contents into his face.

He was up faster than she'd ever seen him move. His hand found her neck, and he forced her backwards, almost lifting her off the ground, slamming her against the wall. His grip tightened, and he stared into her eyes.

"Don't you ever do that again," he snarled, then loosened his hold. His breath came in short bursts. "Don't you... *ever*... do that again."

He relinquished his grip, and she ran from him, up the stairs and into the bedroom, where she jammed a chair against the door, propping it under the handle. The wind wailed through the broken window, billowing the one remaining curtain, but she didn't care.

Becky got into bed, pulled the duvet over her head, and lay there, wide awake, until eventually, hours later, sleep welcomed her into its dark embrace.

11

John had left for work by the time she woke the next morning.

She felt drained — physically and emotionally — from her outburst, and wanted to lie in bed for the rest of the day. Or possibly week. But she had the tapes to pick up, and that was more important than practicing self-care. It was more important than *anything*.

The chair still leaned against the door, and Becky assumed John hadn't tried to enter during the night. Downstairs, she found her laptop on the living room table with a note attached.

Becky, it read in his messy cursive. *I'm sorry about last night. So so sorry. I worry about you that's all, and like you I sometimes lose control of my emotions. Seeing you smashing our window with a golf club and ranting about people hiding in wardrobes made me scared. I hope you can forgive me.*

I've called in a favour and a friend is coming tonight to fix the window. It'll be in the evening so you won't have to deal with him. I'll be there. In the meantime take care of yourself. Have a bath, watch some TV, whatever it takes to ~~calm down~~ destress.

We spoke about you having a spa day why don't you look and see if theirs any available this week?

I love you,

J

Becky read the missive, then re-read it. At first, she was furious, and not just at the spelling and punctuation. The emotional manipulation was off the fucking charts.

"Like you, I sometimes lose control of my emotions," she said aloud, as if his actions had been justified. Then all that talk of how worried he was… she considered tearing the note to shreds. She had hidden in bed all night, fearful for her safety after he had wrapped his hand around her throat and threatened her. Should she leave now, while he was away?

And go where?

She had no friends, no family other than Flora, and frankly, she'd rather live under a bridge than with her sister. There was nowhere to turn. And anyway, the more she thought about it, perhaps John was right? *Was* she a child? Did she act up, and need someone to look after her, to keep her in line?

"No, he's messing with my mind," she said, speaking the words aloud to convince herself of the truth.

But he had never done anything like that before. It could be a one-off. His work was demanding, and she tried to imagine her reaction if she walked into the bedroom and found him smashing the place up. She'd be horrified.

She'd be afraid.

But it wasn't her fault! There *had* been someone there. Absolutely one-hundred percent, no doubt. And she would explain that to him tonight, over dinner.

Or was it best not to? Was drawing a veil over last night and forgetting the whole experience the sensible option? It would be *easier* than having a difficult conversation. Less mentally taxing.

Were all relationships so complicated? From what she saw on television and in the movies, couples argued all the time. People were constantly fighting and making up. So why did it feel so wrong?

"John's a good man," she told herself. "He's always been supportive of me." And was he right about her behaviour since her diagnosis? Had she changed? Probably. All the books she read told her to try dropping the act she put on to get through the day to be more — as they always put it — authentically autistic. *Unmasking,* they called it.

The only problem was people liked her even *less* when she let her guard down. She didn't consider herself an unlikeable person. Challenging, sometimes. But not horrible.

Her phone alarm beeped, signalling the arrival of eight o'clock. The final two tapes would soon be ready for collection. A glimmer of excitement flickered through her, and she folded the note and tucked it into her pyjama pocket. She would talk with John about it. Not tonight, but soon.

One day.

If it ever happened again, though she doubted it would.

He said he *loved* her.

Hell, she had it in writing.

~

Inevitably, *Andy's Laser Emporium* was closed.

She should have known better than to trust that man.

Fool me once, shame on you, she thought. *Fool me twice, shame on me.* It was five-past-ten — her bus had been delayed by road works — and the CLOSED sign was lit and all the lights were off. Where *was* he? She needed a pick-me-up, and these videos were all that would suffice. As she waited for Andy to turn up, cursing his lack of punctuality, she tried not to think of John's face last night, or the way he had looked at her as if he *hated* her. When it came to reading emotions, she often struggled, but even she knew that John had been apoplectic with rage.

It frightened her, even more than the weird happenings in the bedroom, and she fantasised about leaving him, picturing his face when he arrived home to find her out of his life forever.

But what if, secretly, that would please him? What if he *wanted* rid of her?

Oh, where had it all gone wrong for them?

At ten-thirty, tired of her own jumbled thoughts, Becky peered through the Emporium's murky windows. She tried the door, rattling it in the frame, almost giving up before she noticed the sign said PUSH, not PULL. This time, the door opened.

"Jeez." Had the shop been open all along?

It'd help if he changed the sign and put the lights on.

She entered and navigated the narrow aisles in the semi-darkness. The door behind the counter was half-open.

"Excuse me? I've come to pick up my videos. You said they'd be ready."

A tangy, unpleasant odour from the back room assaulted her nostrils. Becky wrinkled her nose. "Hello? I'm here to pick up my tapes." She glanced over her shoulder, remembering the tall man she had seen the previous day. At the time, she had brushed it off, but after last night, the lingering memory came screaming back in sharp relief. She found the latch for the counter and unhooked it, then lifted the lid and wandered through the back door, praying she wouldn't find the proprietor watching porn and wanking.

Inside, the blinking lights from various electrical gadgets did little to offset the darkness. She fumbled for a light switch, found none, and hugged her arms around her chest. It was freezing in here, and no wonder. Someone had left the back door open.

"Hello?"

She approached the exit, figuring that Andy would be outside emptying the rubbish bins. Her feet slid out from under her, and she crashed to the floor, her fall broken by her backpack. Had the door been left open all night, letting the rain flood in? Struggling to stand in liquid that seemed to coat the entire floor, she wiped her palms on her jeans and continued onwards, shuffling along so as not to fall again. Something soft brushed her face, and she screamed, batting it away. Whatever it was, it was dangling from a hanging lamp shade. It slipped free and splatted to the floor.

"Oh god."

That smell... that awful smell...

She walked expeditiously towards the open door, her toes kicking a wooden and weighty object on the ground. She looked down, and, in the dim light that crept through the exit, saw it was the door.

Someone had broken in. Oh god, what if they'd taken her tapes? She reached the doorway, stepping outside and taking deep breaths to rid herself of the stench. Hanging her head, she glanced down at herself... at the dark, crimson stains on her jeans and trainers... at her blood-smeared hands...

She didn't want to go back inside.

She wanted to run away, to go home and strip off and take a shower, to throw her stained clothes in the bin, to *burn* them. But she *had* to investigate. Someone might need to call the police.

And so Becky turned back, standing in the doorway and running her bloody hands over the wall until she located the light switch. She clicked it on, and stood, immobile, as she gazed upon the wretched display of human remains spread across the room.

There was blood on the floor and on the walls, and in the middle of the room was something in the shape of a man, though it was flat, as if ground into a fine paste. The clothes were torn, the skin ragged and split, while the internal organs were strewn around like debris in the aftermath of a party.

Dazed, Becky pulled her phone from her pocket and tried to dial 9-9-9. She got two digits in before she dropped to her knees, turned her head, and vomited.

12

The police officer glanced up from his notepad. "So you were there around, say, six-thirty last night?"

"Yes, that's right," said Becky. She sat in the back of the cruiser, trying not to fidget by watching the easy flow of the officer's hands as he jotted down her answers. "He was digitally transferring my videotapes, and I went to pick them up."

"And you spoke to Mr Malcolm?"

She nodded.

"How was he acting?"

Christ, she had gone over this already. After calling in her grisly find, she had waited outside for the police to arrive, then answered their damn questions. Why did she have to go over it again?

"I told you, he was fine. He said my videos weren't ready, but they would be this morning, which is why I came here at ten — well, five-past-ten because the bus was slow — to collect them. I found him like..." — she gestured vaguely — "...well, like *that*."

"So you just walked behind the counter when there was no one there?"

Her mind raced, and she tried to relax, but all she could think about was Jason Statham. The cop interviewing her was the spitting image of the famous action movie star. They shared the same strong jawline and short, balding hairstyle, and Becky couldn't help admiring the perfect shape of the officer's head.

God, he could be Statham's stunt double.

Throughout her life, she had picked up various obsessions, from horses and ponies as a child, to ancient Egypt and the Brit-pop band Pulp as a teenager. Sometimes these fixations lasted a few weeks, other times years. For the last decade, one of her key special interests — as they were known in autistic circles — had been the films of Jason Statham. She loved the comfort they brought her. Even the bad ones, like *Chaos*.

"Mrs Sharp, are you listening?"

"Sorry, what did you ask?"

His brow creased. All that was missing was Statham's bulging head vein.

"I said, you went behind the counter and no one was there. Is that correct?"

Disappointingly, he didn't *sound* like Jason Statham.

"That's, uh, right," she said. "I was looking for the owner. For Andy. I saw the door was open, and I knew that's where he—"

"And who was this tall man you mentioned to my colleague?"

"What man?"

"You said someone else had been in the shop yesterday."

"Yes, well, I'm not sure about that. I saw someone, but

Andy didn't. He was following me. I'd seen him that morning in the burnt-down building across the street. Do you think he did it?"

"Maybe," said the officer. "You've not given us much of a description to go on." He pocketed his notepad and leaned against the car door. "So, Mrs Sharp, it appears you were the last person to see Andrew Malcolm alive."

She pondered this. "No, that's incorrect. Whoever killed him is the last person to see him alive."

"Sure," smiled the cop. "But you were the first person to find him dead?"

Becky said nothing. Her head ached.

"Quite a coincidence, isn't it?"

She didn't like this man. If only it was Jason Statham in the car with her, then things would be different. Jason always championed the underdog. He stood up for them. He protected them. Without him, she would have to defend *herself*.

"I don't think that's coincidental at all. If Andy never left the shop after I'd spoken to him, how could anyone else have seen him, other than his killer?"

"That's precisely what I mean."

"What are you inferring? That I killed him?"

The cop looked her over. "You're covered in his blood."

"I told you, I slipped, PC..."

"*Detective Constable* Larkin," he said, emphasising his lofty title.

"Okay, *Detective Constable* Larkin. I slipped. If I had killed the proprietor, for whatever reason, why would I phone the police? It makes no sense."

"I find crime rarely does. But, off the record, no, I don't think you did it. Whoever killed Mr Malcolm must have been strong. Ridiculously strong. The mess they made..." He shook his head, and Becky couldn't tell if he was appalled or impressed. "I apologise for all the questions. It's part of the job." He tapped his temple and smiled thinly. "Have to gather all the facts."

"It's okay. Can I go now?"

"In a second." He produced a card from his pocket and held it out to her. "This is my personal number. If you remember anything else, or if you see that tall man again, call me."

She took the card, leaving bloody fingerprints around the edge.

"Or just call me," he said, "if you want to talk."

She looked from the card to his face and back again. Was he flirting with her? "I'd better go. My husband will be waiting."

His expression changed, and she thought that for once, she had read his intentions correctly.

Forty-four years, and I'm finally getting good at this!

"Of course," he said. "And I'm sorry, but we'll have to keep your tapes for now. They're evidence."

"I understand." She exited the vehicle and walked from the cruiser, letting the rain soak her bloodstained clothes. There was no doubt about it. The policeman fancied her. The policeman who resembled a young Jason Statham *fancied* her.

She pocketed his card.

What a pity you're married.

To an abuser.

She winced. That wasn't fair. Last night was a one-off.

Once is once too often.

She knew that, but she also knew John, and had known

him for over fifteen years. In that time, he had never... oh, what was the point? She was only arguing with herself. Still, it was preferable to thinking about the back room of *Andy's Laser Emporium*. In a twisted way, she was glad Andy's remains were in such a state. It made the macabre scene less real. Had he looked like a normal corpse, she might have been more upset. But instead, he was an avant-garde presentation of a man. A Picasso, a piece of outsider art.

Like *Rumplejack*.

Ah yes, her videos.

I'm sorry, but we'll have to keep your tapes for now, the handsome detective had said. When Becky played the conversation back in her mind, he growled in Jason Statham's gravelly voice. *They're evidence.*

"Yeah, sure," said Becky, as she rounded the corner in her bloodstained jeans and mingled with the early morning crowd, most of whom paid her scant attention. She unzipped her backpack and looked inside. There, tucked beneath Grumpus her plush penguin, were the two remaining tapes.

Fully aware that the police would declare the area a crime scene, Becky had searched the room for her videos. Before placing them in her bag, she had looked for CCTV cameras and found none. Then, after dialling the emergency services, she had worked on what she would say to the police, planning her script to the smallest detail. She had even asked them about whether she could look for her tapes, safe in the knowledge the answer would be a stern no.

She grazed the videos with her fingertips, then zipped up her bag.

I'm a criminal mastermind.

She laughed at that, and still no one paid her any attention. This was Leith, and weirdos were everywhere, especially at this time of day. She checked her watch. The bus would be here soon, a bus that would take her to her next destination, the only place she could think of archaic enough to still have a video recorder.

Her dad's care home.

13

"Morning, dad."

The old man sat in his chair with his hands folded on his lap, facing the wall. He didn't acknowledge his daughter's presence. The lady at reception had warned her he was having one of his off-days. Becky was familiar with them. On those days, which rolled around more frequently than ever, he would sit quietly in his own little world, paying no heed to his surroundings. It wasn't uncommon for him to experience spells like this before the dementia took hold, but back then, it was possible to shake him from his stupor.

"I brought some videos. Want to watch one?" She laid her backpack on the chair and wheeled a trolley out from the corner of the room. A fourteen-inch telly balanced on the top shelf, connected to a Hitachi VHS recorder that had been kicking around in the family for over thirty years. Growing up, Becky had used the machine to watch tapes of her mother's TV shows, and running her hands over the chunky buttons sent a tingle of sadness through her. She plugged it into the wall and the video recorder whirred into life.

"Hard to believe this thing still works," she said to her dad. "They don't make 'em like this anymore, that's what you always said."

She ejected a tape from the machine — Clint Eastwood's heartwarming tale of orangutan friendship, *Every Which Way But Loose* — and laid it to one side. From the videos in her backpack, she selected one and slotted it into the machine with a satisfying *clunk*.

All the while, her father stared dead ahead. Becky hit PLAY, and shuffled across the carpet to her dad's chair, crossing her legs and leaning her head on the armrest.

PROPERTY OF GOLDEN THISTLE TELEVISION read a title card, which jittered up and down like it was caught in an earthquake. The screen went black, and Becky smiled. It had been a long time since she and her dad had watched telly together, and in the act of doing so, all her recent troubles faded into the background.

"Let's go back,
To Rumplejack,
We've been away too long."

The show started, and Becky was immediately struck by the improvement in picture quality. Okay, it wasn't exactly high definition, but it looked like a good, clear VHS image.

"Your friends await,
So don't be late,
To help them sing this song."

The lighthouse appeared, and Becky hoped the intro wouldn't be quite as long as last time. "You remember any of this?"

Her dad just sat there, staring. Then, he frowned.

"Dad? Are you okay?"

The theme song played on.

"Rumplejack, oh Rumplejack, you're never far away.

Rumplejack, oh Rumplejack, I wish that I could stay."

Her dad said nothing, but he was definitely watching. His narrowed eyes focused on the screen.

"Rumplejack," she said. "Does that mean anything to—"

"Shhhh."

"Sorry," she whispered. She had forgotten how he liked to watch his films in total silence.

The episode opened similarly to the previous one. The long walk to the lighthouse, the endless trudge up the stairs, though thankfully the unnerving subliminal edits of the dark figure were absent.

Once more, the woman with the burnt face took a seat on the lighthouse gantry, and fed a string of sausages to the pug hand puppet. Not a word was spoken, and the episode soon cut to an outdoor public swimming pool. The pool was empty of both water and people. Dead leaves were piled along the bottom, and the camera held its unblinking gaze for several minutes.

Her dad mumbled something inaudible.

"What was that?" she asked.

"I think I've seen this one."

Her heart leaped. "Oh yeah? I found these videos in the wall, dad. The wall of our house. *Your* house. Do you remember putting them there?"

A glimpse of colour on the screen drew her attention. A woman in a red bathing suit entered the frame. She moved unsteadily to the edge of the pool, like a newborn foal learning to walk.

"Please," she said. *"Please don't."*

"Who's she talking to?" asked Becky. Her father didn't answer.

The woman in the bathing suit tottered over to a ladder

that led to a diving board. *"Please, I'm begging you. I'll do anything you want."*

She started to climb, pausing partway up to look at someone offscreen. Then she lowered her head and resumed her ascent.

"What's going on?" Becky turned to her dad, but he was transfixed.

Stop the tape.

The woman reached the diving board and edged across it, the plank bending under her weight. She raised her hands and touched her fingers together, preparing to dive.

Becky stood, and her dad's hand gripped her wrist.

"Leave it," he said.

She stared at his face, then turned back in time to see the woman spring from the board and sail through the air. As she crashed to the bottom of the pool, her arms splintered, her skull shattering on the—

The screen cut away.

Becky's stomach churned, and the image of Andy's mutilated body roared back into her mind. "What the fuck..."

"Language," her father said.

That woman was dead. She had to be. There were no special effects, no sly edits. She had watched a woman kill herself.

The video abruptly cut back, the woman's ruptured cranium filling the frame, her brains leaking across the pool and heading for the drain, all captured in verité-style handheld camera.

Becky shook free of her father. "No, I can't watch this today. Not after—"

"Hello, Mr Boo."

A woman's voice. A voice that was hauntingly, achingly familiar.

"Meredith," said her father.

"Mum," said Becky.

And they were both right.

She was on the television, sitting on a bench with prison bars between her and the camera, the white walls behind her stained red with blood.

The show cut to a ghost, and Becky gasped, though not due to his frightening visage. Rather, the phantom's costume was a white sheet draped over a man's head and shoulders, the black eyes scribbled on with a marker pen. The sheet hung as low as the wearer's waist, and covered nothing of his unclothed lower half. The man's penis and hairy testicles dangled below the sheet.

"Hello, Meredith," said Mr Boo, in the squeaky voice of a grown man trying and failing to imitate a child.

"You have to get me out of here."

Becky saw her father was crying.

"I can't do that," replied the ghost. *"You're safer in here."*

An unforgiving close-up captured her mum's face. *"Mark, I know it's you."*

"Mark's not here. He's gone away, Tommy sent him away. He's not coming back, not ever again. But I'm here, and I'm your friend. Mr Boo is everybody's friend."

"That's my wife," her dad said. "That's Meredith."

Becky held his hand. "I know." She saw the recognition in her father's face, and it broke her heart. It was lovely to have him back, even if she didn't know how long it would last.

"Mark," her mum said. *"Mr Boo... please, find the keys."*

"I can't. I have to keep the door locked night and day."

Her father's grip on her hand tightened. "Keep the door locked night and day, so Tommy can't come out to play," he said, and turned to her. "But someone let him out."

"Dad, who's Tommy?"

He didn't answer. Instead, he raised a trembling arm and pointed at the TV. A doorway filled the screen. "And if you knock on the big wooden door," he said, his voice dropping to a whisper. *"Tommy will gut you like a whore."*

A chill ran down Becky's spine. "What?"

"Tommy will *gut* you like a *whore.*"

His hand clenched over hers. She felt her bones grinding together.

"Dad, stop."

"Tommy will gut you like a whore, Tommy will gut you like a whore."

Becky glanced at the television. Mr Boo stood in front of the door, his dirty arse poking out beneath the sheet.

"Let go, you're hurting me!"

"Tommy will gut you, Tommy will gut you, Tommy will gut you like a whore."

She tried to wrestle her hand free, but he wouldn't release her.

Onscreen, Mr Boo raised a fist.

"Don't do it," her father said. "Don't knock on Tommy's door."

"But who is he?"

He looked at her, looked her right in the eyes. "Rotten Tommy, that's what they called him. They woke him up. *They woke up the devil!*"

Mr Boo rapped his knuckles against the wood, the sound echoing from the mono speaker as if coming from next door, and Becky's father released her. He rose from his chair, staggering forwards and collapsing to his knees.

"Don't do it! Don't do it!" he cried, crawling towards the TV. Becky wrapped her arms around his waist, attempting to restrain him, and he broke free, dragging his legs behind him as he neared the screen. "Don't do it!"

The door opened, and a figure emerged from the void. He wore a black leather smock, fastened by brown straps across the front that reminded Becky of a straightjacket. Because of his immense height, the top of the figure's face was cut off by the screen, but what remained was a horrifying nightmare. His skin was as white as licked-clean bone, yet soft and lumpy, with a misshapen black orifice that appeared to be his mouth, from which leaked a faecal stream of murky blood.

"Tommy!" her father screamed, hurling himself forwards and grabbing the TV trolley, shaking it.

"Dad, stop!" yelled Becky, closing her arms around him, unable to overpower the supposedly feeble old man. "Help me! Someone help!"

Desperate for one of the nurses to hear her and come to her aid, she turned to the door. The handle was moving.

"In here, quick!"

The door groaned open on tired hinges.

"Help!"

Her father wrestled in her arms, reaching for the TV. She glanced at the screen, and saw the pale-faced man raise a scythe, swiping it down towards Mr Boo's neck. It sliced easily through the white sheet, cleaving it in two, a geyser of blood spurting from the fresh wound. Becky turned back to the door.

"Oh my god!" she screamed, as the pale man — *Rotten Tommy, it's Rotten Tommy* — entered, ducking his malformed head to fit through.

The room lit up as something crashed beside her. She screamed and backed away, staring at her father. The television set had toppled from the trolley, and smashed onto the back of his head. Small sparks hissed from the ruined equipment, smoke rising from her father's broken skull as blood seeped across the carpet like an oil spill.

Becky looked up at the pale man, but all she saw was a wide-eyed nurse rushing to her father's side.

"What happened?" the nurse asked. She checked the old man's pulse and called for help.

"I have to go," said Becky, getting to her feet. She reached for her backpack and ran for the door. "I'm sorry, I have to go!"

"Come back here!" the woman shouted after her. "Someone, stop that woman!"

Becky jogged through the empty corridor, passing door after door, confused faces staring at her from within each one, until she came to the stairs and hurtled down them, her mind in torment. She didn't know what had happened, or even where she was.

All she knew was that she had to get out.

PART II

14

Becky hadn't wished to attend her father's funeral.

It wasn't because she didn't love him. She had, dearly. But funerals were difficult for her. She never cried at them, and as the daughter of the deceased, people *expected* her to cry. They damn near demanded it. What they couldn't understand was that she grieved — and suffered — in her own way.

She had barely left the house since that day in the nursing home. John had stepped up to the task, helping Flora make the arrangements, registering the death, even organising taxis for out-of-town relatives. After the minister's address, he gave a speech to the small crowd, and they laughed and cried in all the right places, dabbing their eyes with tissues as Becky sat stony-faced.

She watched John, and though her heart was secretly in turmoil, it also swelled with pride at what he had achieved. Last week's outburst was all-but-forgotten. She sometimes wondered if she misremembered parts of it. Memories could be so unreliable. How much of people's personalities were formed by incorrect assumptions and forgotten moments? John was not a violent man. She must have pushed all the wrong buttons, that was all. He was a good husband. Hell, he and Flora had spent hours together all week sorting the funeral, and she was grateful to them both, even if a tiny, nagging thought told her—

"You okay?" asked Flora, tears rolling down her cheeks. She offered Becky a tissue.

"I'm fine, thanks." Dammit, she should have taken one and at least pretended. Expressing certain emotions never came easily to her. Anger and happiness were no problem. She understood those perfectly, which was unsurprising considering she had spent the first twenty years of her life vacillating between the two. But sadness? That one she had never mastered. Not that she never felt sad. On the contrary, she often did, and quite disastrously so, but she found it tough to tell the difference between tiredness and jealousy and confusion, and even hunger.

After the funeral, once the remaining mourners had mumbled their goodbyes and wished Becky and John and Flora well, the three sheltered beneath umbrellas as the moody grey sky rumbled above them.

"Thanks again," said Becky, drawing on a cigarette and fighting with a wind that threatened to turn her brolly inside out. "To both of you."

"That's alright," said Flora. "How you holding up?"

"Not bad, I guess. Unlike mum, at least we know dad's dead."

"Becky!"

Flora's indignant tone suggested she should keep quiet, but it was true. Their mother's disappearance had left a gaping hole in both their lives, whether Flora admitted it or not. With their dad, there was a finality. He was dead, and soon he'd be buried, and she knew exactly where to come whenever she felt like visiting. There was no mystery to his passing.

Not one she cared to share, anyway.

John wrapped a protective arm around her. "It's best we head home."

"No," she said, "I'm not ready. Think I'm gonna take a walk and clear my mind."

"If you're sure," said John. "I'll drop Flora off on the way. How long do you think you'll be?"

She shrugged. "Couple of hours."

"Okay. You take it easy, now." He kissed her on the cheek, their umbrellas bumping together, and then John and Flora walked briskly to the car beneath a darkening sky, their polished shoes splashing in the puddles.

Becky watched them go, and waved as the car rode by. Rain pounded off the windows, and she couldn't tell if they waved back or not.

"Hey, how are you?"

Fuck, who was this now? She thought all the mourners had left. Bristling with irritation, she turned to find Jason Statham standing before her.

"Oh my god," she gasped, then realised it was the cop from the electronics store. "Oh, it's you," she said, unable to hide the disappointment in her voice. What was his name again?

Detective Constable Larkin.

Yes, that was it. DC Larkin.

"Sorry," the detective said. "Did I startle you?"

"I thought I was alone."

He stared at her from behind dark sunglasses that only emphasised his resemblance to Statham, and her cheeks flushed from anger or embarrassment, she wasn't sure.

"Nice service," he said. "Your husband gave a moving speech."

"Why are you here?" She knew she sounded rude, but it was a damn good question, and it deserved to be asked. "Checking up in case I've killed anyone else? Like my father?"

He appeared lost for words. "Look, I... uh, maybe this was a bad idea. I'm only here to pay my respects."

"I've already given my statement about my dad," she said, instantly regretting bringing *that* minor catastrophe up. She prayed he hadn't read it.

"Yeah, I read it," he said.

Fuck. Fuck shit fuck.

Thankfully, he moved on quickly. "Your father's death was an accident, Mrs Sharp. We're not treating anyone as a suspect."

"Well, I don't appreciate being accosted at his funeral."

"I didn't mean to accost you. I only wanted to talk." He smiled at her. It was a difficult smile to read. "Is there somewhere indoors we could go?"

"I'm happy out here. I was about to take a walk, actually."

"Mind if I accompany you?"

"Yes, I do."

He nodded. "Okay, I'm sorry. I'll leave you alone. But please, there's something I have to know." He shoved his hands in his pockets and looked around, as if checking to see if anyone was listening. "It's about that man you saw. When you gave your statement, you told the officer a tall man with a white face entered the room right as your father died."

Becky's toes curled in embarrassment at the recollection. She had made a terrible scene that day, and the thought of the whole humiliating ordeal, during which she had ranted and screamed about her dad and Rumplejack and her autism, before shutting down completely, haunted her.

"I did say that, yes."

The detective removed his sunglasses and wiped the rain from them in a futile gesture. "Was it... was it the same man you saw in the electronics shop?"

Becky considered her answer carefully. There was something disarming about this policeman, and not only his uncanny resemblance to her favourite actor. He seemed... nervous?

"Yes," she said. "I think it might have been." It wasn't quite the truth — she *knew* it was the same man — but it also wasn't a lie.

"And you called him Tommy?"

Again, she chose her words with caution. "That's what my dad called him."

The detective looked thoughtful. "If you see him again—"

"I have your number. Now, if you'll forgive me, Mr Martin, I have to be—"

"It's Larkin," he interrupted.

"What?"

"You called me Martin, but my name's Larkin. Gregor Larkin."

"Oh. I guess you remind me of someone," she said, though she declined to mention he reminded her of Jason Statham's character in *The Transporter* series, Frank Martin. "Anyway, if we're done here, I'll be on my way."

She turned, leaving the detective standing in the rain, and began to walk. Why the hell had he—

"I've seen him, too," he called after her.

Becky froze. Should she keep walking? She glanced over

her shoulder at the detective, trying to gauge the sincerity in his voice.

"No, you haven't," she said.

"He's tall."

"I already told you that."

"Yeah, but *real* tall. Easily seven feet, maybe closer to eight. He wears black, like a robe or something, but made from old, tarnished leather." Larkin took a breath. "But his face is pure white. Whiter than anything I've ever seen, with no defined features. At first I thought it was a mask, but—"

"Okay, I get it, you read my statement. There's nothing you've said that you couldn't find in there. Isn't this... *what do you call it*... entrapment?"

"I watched *Rumplejack,* Mrs Sharp," he said.

"You couldn't have, you liar," she shot back. "I took the —" She caught herself in time, one second before admitting to her crime. "I mean, I took, ummm, I..."

"I know you have the tapes. I turned the place upside-down looking for them, and couldn't find any videos except for some vintage pornography belonging to the owner. But one of yours had been transferred. I found it on the computer, and I watched it. I thought it might be relevant to the case. But ever since..."

Becky moved close enough to hold her umbrella over the pair of them. "What do you want from me?"

"I don't know. It sounds crazy, but... shit, I don't know what I'm trying to say. I need those other tapes, Becky."

"They're gone. I threw them away."

"I can get a warrant if I have to."

She smiled at him. "Thank you for threatening me at my dad's funeral, you bastard." She took a step back. "I'd suggest you don't watch *Rumplejack* again. And if you see Tommy... stay away from him. For your own sake. *Good day,* detective," she said, as she strode towards the cemetery gate. Why had she lied about throwing the tapes away? He was only trying to help her. Wasn't he? It was true he could get a search warrant, but she didn't think he would. How would he justify it to his superiors? That he suspected she was harbouring forty-year-old recordings of a fictional character who *might* be a murderer?

No, the videos belonged to her. More importantly, the tapes *knew* they did, and would not allow anyone to come between them. A week prior, after she had given her calamitous statement to the police, Becky had — in a depressive funk, and reeling from shock — tried to destroy the two remaining tapes. She had smashed one against the table, and hadn't cracked the plastic. Throwing another from the window yielded similar results, and only after she attacked the videotape with one of the workers' mallets did she give up.

They were unbreakable.

By way of retaliation, she had refused to watch them, choosing instead to go to bed and remain there indefinitely, while a single thought tormented her every waking moment.

What if she hadn't visited her father and shown him the tape?

As she walked from the cemetery, she thought about the deaths and the visions and the endless questions from the police. Her synapses were fried, and a large part of her wanted to return home and crawl back into bed forever, where she could dream about moving abroad and living off-the-grid with no one to bother her. But during the funeral, she had come to a realisation.

She had no choice but to watch the videos.

For whatever was on them had taken not only her

mother, but her father, too. Though she didn't understand how, or why, she was convinced she would find the answers on those damn videotapes.

"Fuck it," she said, opening the eBay app on her phone. She found a cheap VHS machine, bought it, and paid the extra seven pounds for next day delivery.

She would watch the remaining tapes, and nothing — not some detective, and certainly not Rotten fuckin' Tommy — would stop her.

15

DC Larkin arrived at the police station at eleven. He nodded a passing greeting to the desk clerk, who was listening patiently as an elderly woman ranted about her neighbours playing their music too loud, and carried on down the winding, antiseptic corridors that led to his office. He was situated on the second floor, near the rear of the building, which gave him a pleasant view from his window of Edinburgh's extinct volcano, Arthur's Seat. It hadn't erupted in over three-hundred-million years, but sometimes Larkin wished it would, and today was one of those days.

He locked the door and booted up his PC. As it began installing updates for what felt like the tenth day in a row, his gaze settled on the window.

That was where he had first seen him.

Tommy.

Before Larkin had even watched the video, Tommy had been out there, standing in the carpark and staring up at the window like a phantasm, blood dripping from his hammer into a shallow pool by his feet.

The computer updates finished, and he selected the file marked SHARP_VIDEO_2.

Rotten Tommy was what the characters in *Rumplejack* called him, and what a monumentally fucked-up show it was. Thorough analysis of the video told him beyond reasonable doubt that the deaths — murders, even — in the show were real. His colleagues had proved harder to convince. They laughed it off, pointing out that if snuff films existed, they likely wouldn't have opening and closing credits, or feature puppets dancing to disco music. Larkin conceded the point, but they hadn't seen the ghoulish spectre that haunted him, always lurking at a distance as if waiting for the right moment to strike.

His discussion with Becky Sharp had gone poorly. He needed her on his side. Who else would believe him? Absently, he double-clicked the file and let the first episode commence. How many times had he watched it already? Twenty? Thirty? Enough that on each viewing, he noticed subtle, unexplainable changes. Characters hesitating during dialogue, or glancing at the camera, or — on one occasion that had never repeated — sneezing. The only elements that remained unaltered were the subliminal frames of Tommy, his doughy white head forever turned away from the camera's unwavering gaze.

Larkin clicked along the timeline until he neared the end of the last episode, which usually fell around minute one-seventy-five, depending on how much the episodes distorted themselves. In the final shot, the burnt woman sat alone in the disco, the lights strobing and changing colour to the soundtrack of a single low piano note hammered repeatedly. Over this bizarre tableaux, the end credits rolled. As with every episode, interference and tracking problems plagued the closing minutes, rendering the credits almost impossible to read.

"Almost," said Larkin. He picked up his trusty legal pad and pen, and began moving through the credits frame-by-fucking-frame, squinting at the screen until he found a name he could just-about read. He scribbled it down and smiled thinly. "But not impossible."

∼

Becky signed for the special delivery of the VHS recorder at nine-fifteen, but had to wait two more hours for Amazon to deliver the SCART to HDMI adaptor she had ordered. By the time it arrived, the recorder was unpacked and plugged in and ready to go. It smelt of cigarette smoke and the 1990s.

A call had come through to her landline, going straight to voicemail. It was the producer of a show she was writing a script for, an STV drama about a young policewoman facing corruption in the force. The producer expressed his sympathy for her recent circumstances, but as she was already a fortnight past the deadline, he wondered — in a tone simultaneously genial and threatening — if she had any updates on when the script would be ready.

She didn't, and so she waited for the voicemail to end and deleted the recording. Not wishing to be disturbed any further, she unplugged the telephone. Who the hell used landlines these days? Call her mobile or — better yet — email and don't call at all.

She inserted a tape into the machine, which hungrily gobbled it up to a chorus of aggressive whirrs and clicks. The LCD blinked 00:00 at her, and she pushed the button.

This was the last tape.

The first had contained one episode of Rumplejack and

a lot of static. The second was in a VHS player in her dad's nursing home. Would they still have it? Or had they already thrown out his belongings and given the room to someone else? The nursing home was a business, and businesses were not known for their sentiment.

Never mind. She had two of the three tapes, and that would have to suffice. If she could face returning to the scene of her father's death, she might pop in this week. For now, she would make do.

Becky steeled herself and reached for the recorder. Hugging Grumpus, her cuddly penguin, to her chest, she hit PLAY and started to watch.

∾

Dead.

They were all *dead*.

Rain pattered against the window as Larkin stared at his computer monitor. How could everyone who worked on *Rumplejack* be dead?

Identifying them via the Internet Movie Database had been simple, as most were television veterans with a considerable body of work. The cameraman had been an assistant on *Doctor Who* in the seventies, the composer seemed to specialise in advertisement jingles, while the boom operator's most notable credits were a few episodes of BBC sitcom *Some Mothers Do 'Ave 'Em*.

And all, according to the internet, were long deceased.

"Can't all be," Larkin grunted, though only two names remained on his list, and his current search — for someone listed as 'Researcher' — revelled in the ungoogleable moniker of John Smith. Luckily, the final name was a safer bet. Surely there couldn't be too many Quintin Horsham-Blakes knocking about?

Larkin typed the name into IMDB, and there he was. Unlike the others, there was even a photo of Horsham-Blake, a small image with a reddish cast like a faded Polaroid. He looked to be in his forties when the photo was taken, with a smart, military-style haircut and oversized glasses. As was the case with every name he had searched, there was no mention of *Rumplejack* on Horsham-Blake's filmography.

"Wait a minute," said Larkin, as he chewed the tip of his pen. He opened a new tab and input the man's name into Wikipedia. The office lights flickered, and he ignored them as he scanned Horsham-Blake's Wiki entry. It gave his date of birth, but...

"Holy shit." Larkin's lips curled into a smile. "You're not dead, you old bastard."

He tried to contain his excitement. The internet was notoriously unreliable, and the director may have been deceased for decades, but there were no death dates listed anywhere online.

Outside, the rain picked up, hammering the window. Larkin accessed the Police Scotland database, typing the wrong password in his excitement. Grumbling profanities, he logged in correctly and proceeded to search for Quintin Horsham-Blake. He would input *all* the names, of course, but right now, Horsham-Blake was his—

The lights extinguished, plunging the office into semi-darkness. The computer, too, died.

"Dammit!" Larkin hammered his fist against the desk, causing a photograph of his cat, Marcy, to fall facedown. "What's going on out there?" he shouted, rising from his chair.

He tried the light switch to no avail, flicking it off and on again, then barged into the door, forgetting it was locked. Rubbing his shoulder, he unlatched the door and stepped into the darkened corridor. Wasn't there supposed to be a backup generator or—

"Oh, shit."

A single light at the far end of the corridor offered the only source of illumination. Beneath it lurked the silhouette of a tall man, *obscenely* tall, his head scraping the ceiling, his immense bulk filling the width of the passageway.

"Who is that?" Larkin asked, more out of duty than curiosity. He knew who the man was. And for the first time in many years, he felt the chill grip of terror constricting his lungs.

It's not real, it's a dream.

Bollocks it was.

"This is a restricted area. Please identify yourself."

Use his name. You already know it.

But he couldn't. It was too bizarre, too impossible. Larkin turned to his office door, considering whether or not to fetch a weapon. When he looked back, the man was coming towards him. He closed the distance with enormous strides, the single light source catching the outline of the metal hammer clutched in his hand.

Larkin remained frozen with indecision. He needed a gun, but he didn't have one. Thanks to Scotland's strict firearm safety laws, the police force's guns were all safely locked away in the basement for special circumstances.

"Stop right there."

His shaky voice was unrecognisable. Fifteen years of law enforcement, and somehow the rapidly advancing character from a children's TV show was what broke him. Regaining control of his legs, Larkin stumbled backwards to the next office, flinging the door open and finding nobody inside.

Still, the big man advanced.
You know his name.
Tommy.
Call to him.
Rotten Tommy.
Beg for your life.

It would do no good. Larkin understood this. He could do nothing but flee, and when the big man smacked his hammer into the wall and a river of dark blood seeped out, that was precisely what he did.

∾

With her heart palpitating, Becky knelt before the TV and nibbled on the skin around her fingers. The screen stayed black for so long that she had to find two AAA batteries in the kitchen drawer — the Useful Drawer, she called it — and put them in the remote control in order to fast-forward the tape.

"Come on, come on," she muttered impatiently, squeezing Grumpus in anticipation. It couldn't be blank! Where was the timecode, or the PROPERTY OF GOLDEN THISTLE card?

There.

A picture.

She hit play, then rewound, eager not to miss a second of... a home video? She scowled in disappointment. This wasn't *Rumplejack*. This was a smeary image of a beach, clearly shot using a consumer-level camcorder. The picture jerked clumsily in the operator's inexpert hands, panning across the undeniably pretty landscape until—

"Oh my god," she said.

On the TV, her mum lay face-down on a towel, wearing

sunglasses and a pink bikini, her head tilted towards the camera.

"Stop filming me," she laughed. *"If you get sand in that thing, it'll break."*

"I'm just checking it's working."

"Don't be fooled by the sunglasses. I can see you recording my bum."

Her mum was correct. Her arse filled the frame, her dad zooming in to immortalise the posterior. There was a date in the corner. August twelfth, 1984. A few months prior to her mum's disappearance.

"I'm not recording," her dad lied.

"So why is the red light on?"

"The what?"

"Dad," said Becky, embarrassed to be watching this private moment. She shook her head and pressed the fast-forward button. There were long, panning shots of the beach — the analogue image looked awful on a fifty-inch Smart TV, the colours bleeding into each other — sound-tracked by the dull roar of the ocean and the distant caw of gulls. The camera picked out her mum capering in the surf, followed by another extended stretch of blank screen.

"Why were you hidden in the wall?" asked Becky. There was nothing weird about this tape. Nothing disturbing, or untoward. "Innocuous," she said to Grumpus, for that was the best word to describe it. A new image appeared. A living room that Becky recognised. For how could she not? It was the room next door.

"Wow," she said, as her four-year-old self stood against the curtains, clutching Grumpus the penguin and singing a ghastly off-key rendition of *Jingle Bells* for the benefit of the camera. Her hair was newly cut into a horrible pudding-bowl style, and she was missing several baby teeth. "I was tone deaf," she said, which held true to this day. The-little-girl-she-used-to-be finished the song and ran from the room without a word, while the operator — her dad, most likely — whip-panned after her. She stopped at a wicker moses basket, leaned in and kissed her baby sister, and hurried from the room with her penguin.

"Aye, goodnight to you too, sweetheart," said her dad, and her mum laughed. He spun the camera over to her, struggling to focus. *"How do you work this bloody thing...?"*

Becky smiled. Give her father a hacksaw or a wrench, and he became a one-man *A-Team*. But hand him a piece of technology, and he was lost. It had never changed. All at once, the gravity of her father's passing hit her.

She paused the tape.

Never again would she go round to set his digital alarm clock an hour forwards or backwards, or tune the channels on his telly. Her father was gone, *forever*. But thanks to this video, he could — like the tapes of her mother's television work — live on in her memory, immortalised on film. Well, video, at least. The technologically inferior medium.

Becky smiled at how appropriate that was, and resumed the tape.

∽

Before Larkin rounded the corner, he glanced down the darkened corridor. He couldn't see Tommy, but the laborious pounding of the man's feet echoed in dreadful harmony with the hammering of Larkin's overworked heart.

"Help!" he shouted, embarrassed by his inability to defend himself. "I need backup!" No one answered, or perhaps no one heard his cries. In a building where hundreds of people passed through every day, he was absurdly alone. Reason told him this couldn't be happening, but reason was full of shit. This was no dream. As a teenager, Larkin had — like most kids at the time — experimented with mushrooms, and in his early twenties, he had tried LSD. He recalled the hallucinations, and could still picture the visions, but they were nothing like this. What he was experiencing was reality at its coldest and most alien, and he had no choice but to accept it. Life was a series of inconsistencies and contradictions and bizarre, happenstance coincidences, and people unblinkingly accepted them without question every day. How was this — when boiled down to its base essence — any different?

Larkin sped up, racing past doors with frosted glass panels that would offer no resistance to Tommy's hammer. He needed safety, he needed security, he needed…

The fire exit.

He spotted it, and rammed his hip against the release bar. As he burst through, a high-pitched alarm erupted from above. That was no problem. He wasn't trying to *hide* from Tommy. Just put a barrier between them.

He rushed into the damp stairwell and slammed the door, looking for the medical supply box that was positioned on each level. It was there in case of emergencies, containing bandages and provisions for anyone trapped in the station due to a disaster or terrorist attack. Right now, though, he needed it to keep Tommy out. Larkin shoved the box onto its side and wedged it between the door and bannister. He wondered how far the door would open, and soon found out as it thudded against the box and juddered to a halt. Through the narrow gap, Larkin caught a half-glimpse of Tommy's face peering through, though the lack of light hid the ghastliest details. All he could make out were a vast, sunken eye, and Tommy's twisted black grimace.

Larkin stepped back to the stairs, his heel rocking over the edge and almost sending him pitching backwards. Gripping the rail, he watched as Tommy slammed his meaty fists against the metal door. It shuddered under the impact, and a thin crack split the glass front of the supply box in two. It wasn't going to hold. The door
...keep the door locked night and day...
was going to break. In a few seconds
...So Tommy can't come out to play...
Tommy would burst through.

"Shit, shit, shit," said Larkin, unaware he was doing so. He started down the stairs as the door buckled, metal screeching as Tommy bent it backwards.

Ignoring the mounting pressure in his bladder, Larkin ran, descending the staircase in a crazed panic and using the vague hint of light from below to guide him. He reached the last set of stairs and bounded down. The green Fire Exit sign was still illuminated, a lone beacon in the darkness. Larkin took the final four steps in a single leap and ploughed shoulder first into the door that would lead him to safety. He clanged off the metal and staggered backwards.

It wouldn't open.

"No," he grunted, trying again. He rattled the fire exit, slapped his palms against the door, kicked it hard enough to hurt his toes... but it would not budge. Upstairs, metal crashed, the door clattering down the first flight of stairs.

Tommy had broken through.

"Help me!" roared Larkin. He battered the door with his fists. "Somebody help me!"

Ponderous footsteps reverberated wickedly throughout the stairwell, bouncing off the walls in a maddening crescendo. Tommy was in no rush.

"Help me! Fucking help!"

But it was useless. Nobody could hear him. He turned, and in the feeble glow of the exit sign, he saw Tommy's hulking frame lurch down the stairs, the metal hammer screeching over the handrail with a tormented wail. Larkin pressed his spine to the exit, his palms flat against the door, and tried to convince himself it was all a twisted dream, that he would wake up any minute now, that... that...

Tommy took the last step. He reached for Larkin, who — frozen in pitiful fear — let the big man's icy fingers close over his neck. The hammer glinted, basking in the exit sign light as Tommy raised it high, clumps of hair attached to the bell by murky, dried blood.

Larkin closed his eyes and waited for death.

∽

It was a Christmas party.

Becky tore her eyes from the screen and glanced around the room, ashamed of how little the decor had changed in the forty years since the video was filmed.

Onscreen, dozens of revellers in paper hats and Christmas jumpers were crammed into the living room. Johnny Mathis crooned over the speakers, the record popping and crackling as her dad mingled with the crowd, turning the camera onto random partygoers and asking them if they were having a good time.

"Absolutely," said a man wearing glasses and a bushy moustache, a cigarette clamped between his fingers. "It's a marvellous gathering!"

Another man, also with glasses and a moustache — Becky supposed it was the fashion of the time — offered two drunken thumbs up, before stumbling away to skulk beneath the mistletoe.

A permed woman in a crimson frock grinned and kissed the man next to her.

"*Jackie!*" said her father. "*Are you having a good Christmas?*"

"*The best!*" the woman replied. She took a draw on a cigarette, her nails painted blood red. "*Where's Meredith? I've not seen her since we arrived.*"

"*Oh, she's not feeling well. Been working all month, you know.*"

Becky glanced at the date in the bottom corner. December twenty-sixth, 1984. The day before she was last seen, according to the poster.

None of the names or faces rang a bell. She supposed they were all her mum's acquaintances. Her dad had few close friends, and had never been a sociable man. Even now, filming the party, the camera acted as a buffer between him and the guests. Becky imagined that when her mum went missing, her friends had drifted from the family. That was okay with her, but she wondered if her dad — who never excelled at maintaining relationships — had ever felt lonely.

The party footage went on for another hour, and near the end, her mum made a brief appearance. She looked as beautiful as ever, if thinner than usual, and no amount of makeup could adequately disguise the dark shadows under her eyes. She smiled radiantly and pretended to have fun, but Becky knew something was bothering her. Her own childhood-self made a late cameo, wearing her Care Bears pyjamas and carrying Grumpus the penguin by his flipper, before being promptly ushered back to bed.

"*Oh god, she's so cute,*" a pretty, petite blonde said to the camera afterwards.

"*Aye,*" her dad said, "*that's my wee girl. She's fucking knackered from yesterday.*"

"I bet. Hey, who was that guy she was talking about? Did Meredith finally take my advice and hire a butler?"

Becky leaned forwards, struggling to hear the woman's side of the conversation over the Christmas music in the background.

"What do you mean?" asked her father.

The woman shrugged. She smiled at someone offscreen and said something inaudible.

"Kathy!" her dad said, and the woman turned sharply towards the camera. *"What did Rebecca say?"*

"Huh? Oh, yeah. That guy she was going on about. The man in her room."

Becky's heart almost stopped beating.

"Tommy, she called him. Rotten Tommy." The woman laughed and shook her head. *"It sounds like one of her cuddly animals. It's a funny name for—"*

But her father didn't stick around to hear the rest. Still recording, the camera dropped to his side, turning the image upside down. It shook wildly as he dodged through the crowd.

"Meredith!" he shouted. *"Meredith!"*

"What is it?" her mum replied from somewhere through the din of music and drunken revellers.

"He's found her," was all he said, and then the camera jostled as they ran from the room, fighting their way into the hallway. Her dad was first up the stairs, her mum close behind, captured on the inverted film.

"Becky!" they cried out, sheer desperation in both their voices. *"Rebecca!"*

Upstairs was in darkness, the image breaking up into grainy noise. She heard footsteps, then a *click* as someone hit the light switch.

"What's going on?" asked Becky, not noticing the blood

dribbling down her chin from the finger she was gnawing on.

The camera paused for a few seconds, swinging in her father's hand. *"She's not here,"* he said. *"Check the baby's room."*

At last the camera dropped from his hand, thudding onto the purple carpet of Becky's childhood bedroom. It bounced, landed the correct way up, then fell to the side, tilting the image at a forty-five degree angle. From another room — it felt like another dimension — she heard her parents.

"Flora's fine, she's asleep."

"So where's Becky?"

"I don't fucking know! You check downstairs and the garden, I'll look up here!"

More footsteps as her mum raced down the stairs, doors slamming as her father investigated each room, yet all the camera picked up was the purple carpet and, against the far wall, the lower half of the wardrobe.

"Rebecca!" her dad shouted. *"Where are you? We're not angry, we just want to know you're safe!"*

But there was another sound. Faint, like a half-remembered dream.

A child's voice.

"Keep the door locked night and day, keep the door locked night and day, keep the door locked night and day," said the voice.

Becky knew it was her own.

And when two black, mud-caked boots stomped into frame, she couldn't help herself.

"Run!" she shouted at the screen. "Get out of there!"

The boots stepped towards the wardrobe, leaving filthy prints on the carpet. The wardrobe door opened, the little girl's voice growing louder and faster, like she was praying to a god who wasn't listening.

"Dad!" shouted Becky, inches from the screen. "I'm in the bedroom! Where the fuck are you?"

But in the video, young Becky had fallen quiet. The boots were gone too, and all she could see were the dirty tracks and the open wardrobe.

Then the boots reappeared, walking the opposite direction. They crossed the frame, and a second later, young Becky followed, dragged along the carpet by her ankles, her eyes bloodshot, her jaw slack.

Becky stared at the television screen, screaming for her dad and watching as the unseen force yanked her out of sight, the camera readjusting its autofocus to find Grumpus the penguin lying forgotten and alone on the purple carpet, his beady, black eyes staring lifelessly at her across the intervening decades.

~

Is this death?

Larkin opened his eyes.

This hopeless vacuum, this nothingness... is this hell?

But as his vision adjusted, and he took in the stained wall, and felt the chill of metal against the back of his neck, he realised he was in the fire exit stairwell, sitting on the filthy floor. The crotch of his smart black trousers was wet, and his thighs itched.

Tommy was gone.

"Fuck," he moaned, gripping the rail, his head swimming as he made his way laboriously up the stairs. The door lay on the floor, folded in half in an act of impossible strength. Larkin stepped over it, then peered around the doorframe. The lights were on, the halls empty. Removing his jacket, he bunched it up and held it in front of his damp crotch as he marched back to his office.

There, he closed the door, locked it, and sat.

Shock. He was in shock. He needed to calm down, calm down, calm down.

From his desk drawer, he produced a bottle of Scotch and took a swig, then rubbed at his neck, wincing at the tender flesh. He took his phone from his pocket, switched the camera to selfie mode, and inspected himself. Dark, vicious bruises were already forming on his skin.

"Jesus," he said, a tear rolling down his cheek. "I'm going mad."

16

Flora Tremayne was making love to her sister's husband when the telephone rang. At first she ignored it, but when she glanced at the bedside cabinet and saw it was her sister calling, she knew she had to answer. Becky *never* called.

It must be an emergency.

"Fuck, I have to take this," she said, arching her hips and sliding John out of her.

He grabbed her arse and pulled her back towards his cock. "Come on, I'm almost done."

"Be quiet," she snapped, wriggling free and perching on the edge of the bed, wiping her sweaty hands on the sheets. "It's Becky."

"Shit. What does she want?"

"Shut up for two minutes and I'll find out."

She tapped the button to answer and put Becky on speakerphone. "What is it?"

"Flora? Is that you?"

"Yes." She heard the panic in her sister's voice, and rolled her eyes at John.

"Are you home? I have to show you something. A video, one of the videos I found in the wall."

Flora stole a glance at her lover's stiff cock. "Honey, I'm kinda busy right now."

"No, this can't wait. It's a home movie, and it starts off at a Christmas party in our house, from Christmas 1984. You hear me? Are you there?"

"I'm here."

"Okay, so Christmas eighty-four. That mean anything to you? That's when—"

"What's she on about" whispered John. He relaxed into the pillow, laying a hand on Flora's bare thigh.

"—and then I come down the stairs, and I get sent away to bed, and later, dad's talking to this woman—"

"Uh huh," said Flora, pretending she was listening as John's hand slipped between her legs. "Mhhhhm."

"What's that? Did you say something?"

"Huh?"

John slid two fingers inside her.

"Uhhhh, no, nothing. Go on."

She shook her head and grinned at John. God, this was bad. Was he thinking what she was thinking? With her free hand, she wrapped her fingers around John's rock-hard penis, sliding her grasp up and down his thick shaft.

Shit, was this a new kink she was discovering? She laid the phone on the cabinet and motioned for John to move, then climbed onto the bed on all fours and stuck her arse out. John took the bait. He positioned himself behind her, inserting his cock—

She looked over her shoulder and mouthed, *not that hole.*

"—and then it was just hours of carpet, nothing but carpet. He took me, I think he took me away."

John thrust into her, and she closed her eyes in pleasure. The phone had gone silent.

"Is that all?" asked Flora, unsure of what her sister had been saying.

"Is that not enough? I think it ties in with that video I told you about, the TV show with—"

Becky was still ranting about videos and other dumb bullshit when John shuddered in climax. Flora grimaced. He hadn't been kidding about being nearly done.

"I'm gonna come round and show it to you," Becky said.

Flora felt John's ejaculate dribble down her thighs. "What? You're coming here? Becky, I don't have a video player. It's 2024."

"I bought one, I'll bring it round."

"Don't, please. I don't want to see it. I thought you weren't gonna watch those videos anymore? John said—"

"What did John say? When were you speaking to him?"

Becky's husband leaned over and whispered in her ear, *"Abort the mission."*

Flora giggled.

"Are you still there?"

From somewhere in the room, a song played over tinny speakers. It was Shirley Bassey's theme from *Goldfinger*, and Flora recognised it instantly as John's text message ringtone.

"Shut it off!" she hissed at him.

"Is John with you? Flora, is—"

She killed the call, glaring at John while he rummaged in his discarded clothes for his phone. The ringtone ended as he wrestled it from his trouser pocket.

"It was a text," he said.

"From who?"

"Who do you think?" said John, irritably. "It says, *where are you?*"

"You stupid arsehole. I've told you before to switch that fucking ringtone off. She must have sent it while she was talking to me."

John looked puzzled. "Can you do that?"

"What, two things at once? Yes, we're women." She punched the pillow. "Shit. Now she knows about us."

"No. She *suspects*. That's completely different." John stared up at her, his cock wilting. "Anyway, I thought we were gonna tell her?"

"Not like this, you fucking dolt. And stop pouting, you look like a toddler." She flopped onto the bed, squirming as she sat on a wet patch.

"What are you thinking?" asked John, as helpful as ever.

"I'm thinking we should stop this before it gets any worse. It's going to break her heart."

"Stop? And do what, go back to how things were? I don't think so."

"This is my sister we're talking about. Your *wife,* remember?"

"Don't remind me." He joined her on the bed. "She is *not* the woman I married."

"You're good for her. You brought her out of her shell. She needs someone to love her."

John snorted. "But not me." He squeezed Flora's bare calf. "It's you I love."

"It's my cunt you love."

"That's not true. I love your tits, too."

"Yeah, well," she said. "That's understandable."

"I like a woman who takes care of herself. Ever since the," — he made air quotes with his fingers — *"diagnosis,* it's like she's given up on trying to make me happy. She bums around the house in pyjamas and a hoody."

"She's done that since she was a kid."

"Well, maybe that's the problem? She's a kid. Have you seen how many cuddly toys she keeps on the bed? When we have sex — and let me tell you, it's not often — we have to move those fucking things one-by-one." He massaged Flora's feet. "It's hardly a turn-on."

Flora stretched out as he rubbed her skin. God, he was so good at it. She knew Becky's loss would be her gain. John was a terrific lover, one of the best she'd ever had. She had little interest in him other than his cock, but that cock was a fucking masterpiece. John wanted to divorce Becky and marry *her*. He had told her so, more than once, and Flora had led him on without ever committing, because he made her come consistently, and few men managed that.

"She can't help being autistic," said Flora, utilising her last line of defence against John's intimate caresses.

"And I can't help being in love with you." It was a cheesy line, yet it worked. She lay back and let John run his magic hands over her body. She understood his need for her. Becky was a lot to handle. Too much. She never changed, and quirks that people initially found adorable in her soon gave way to despair when they realised she was like this *all the time*. Perhaps it would be better for everyone if John and Becky separated. That way, her sister could find someone — preferably with a high tolerance for *Lord of the Rings* facts — who loved her for who she truly was.

The more Flora thought about it, the more she realised stealing Becky's husband wasn't an unkind act. It was selfless. She should be proud of herself.

And as John entered her — Christ, she had never met a man who recovered so quickly — she smiled at her benevolent nature.

One day, her sister would thank her for this.

Becky laid the phone down. She considered ringing her sister back, and decided against it. There was no sense making a fool of herself. She had, as usual, got the wrong end of the stick. John wasn't with Flora. And even if he *was*, it would be an innocent visit. He had spent a lot of time with Flora since their dad's death, and doubtlessly knew how greatly it had affected her. He was probably round there comforting her, and keeping it a secret from his wife so as not to worry her.

Or he's fucking her.

True. He was most likely fucking her.

The idea had occurred to her before, often at particularly low ebbs in her mental state. "So, twice a week," she mumbled to herself, gazing at the phone, daring it to ring. She wasn't *stupid*. John's late nights, his weekends away... she had long suspected he was having an affair. Not with her sister, though. Some floozy from work, or an old girlfriend looking to rekindle a forgotten romance... but not her *sister*. God, they were probably together right now, laughing at her and infantilising her, which was the absolute worst. She was autistic, not a moron. Her brain worked perfectly well... it simply worked *differently* from other people's.

Goddammit, why did this have to come up now? When she was really *onto* something? Each tape brought her closer to her missing mother, to potentially solving the mystery of her disappearance, and now she had to deal with *this* shit? She had a right to call them up and—

Her phone rang, and she jumped.

Shit.

This was it. The confrontation. The shouting match, the ultimatums, the lies, the... wait, whose number *was* that?

It was a mobile, but not Flora's or John's. Under any other circumstances, Becky would refuse to answer an unknown caller. But she was so hopped up on adrenaline and stress and two litres of Irn Bru that she jabbed the button without thinking and answered.

"Who is this?"

The voice on the end of the line sounded hesitant. *"Mrs Sharp?"*

"Yes?"

"It's Detective Constable Larkin."

Larkin. Her first thought was, *there's been another murder.* Her second was, *do they think I did it?*

"Mrs Sharp," the detective said. *"We need to talk."*

Something was off. He sounded less... professional than before.

"Mrs Sharp, are you there?"

"I'm here." She glimpsed herself in the mirror, her face ashen. "Is this official police business?"

Another pause. *"No. It's personal."* She heard him swallow. *"Are you free this weekend?"*

She didn't know what to say. What the hell was he asking?

"I'm sorry," he said. *"That sounded strange. But if you'll let me, I'll explain everything. I've found something, Mrs Sharp. I've tracked someone down... and I think it's someone you'll want to meet."*

17

"He's still alive?" asked Becky, fidgeting the salt shaker in her hands.

The grim-faced detective nodded. "He is. The poor bastard's been locked away in a sanatorium since the mid-eighties, and he's approaching ninety, but... aye, he's still alive."

Becky leaned against the soft leather of the booth. She had agreed to meet Larkin at a local bar named The Willow, and found him waiting for her in the corner booth when she arrived. She didn't trust the police, and she certainly didn't trust strange men she had barely spoken to, but when the detective told her he had located the director of Rumplejack, she had signed up to his proposal of a road trip without hesitation. This was the break she had been dreaming of. And anyway, time away from John — and from that damned house — seemed like a first-rate idea.

"So where is he?"

"Up north. Some rancid fleapit called the Beechburn Institute in the Highlands. I did some digging, made some calls. Apparently, he's not spoken to anyone in thirty years, but..."

"He'll speak to me," said Becky. "I know he will."

"That's what I'm banking on."

She studied his face. "Have you seen Tommy again?"

The detective stared at his untouched whiskey glass, as if daring himself to drink. "He almost killed me. Chased me through the station and trapped me in the stairs. I couldn't get away."

"So how did you stop him?"

"I didn't. He was there one second, then he was gone." Larkin tugged his shirt collar down, displaying the bruises on his neck. "He left his mark, though."

"Jesus." Becky sipped her lemonade, the ice cubes rattling together. "So when do we go?"

"You packed?"

She patted her rucksack, which had a change of underwear, some toiletries, a paperback, pyjamas, and Grumpus the penguin inside. "Just my essentials."

He offered her a tired smile. "Then how about right now?"

She thought about John, and about how confused and upset he would feel when he came home and found her gone.

"So what are we sitting around for?" she said. "Let's fucking go."

∾

The drive to the Beechburn Institute took longer than expected. The roads were flooded from the relentless downpours of the past fortnight, and an accident on the motorway caused the traffic to be diverted through country tracks that wound through the landscape like mindless scribbles on a sheet of paper.

They passed the journey with faltering conversation. Becky explained what little she knew about her mother's disappearance, while Larkin talked of his sightings of Tommy and his fruitless search for the surviving crew members.

After, once the initial discussion concluded, she Googled Quintin Horsham-Blake, grappling with the appalling mobile data signal in the north of Scotland. Larkin drove with his jaw set in grim determination, stopping only once to fill the tank and pick up sandwiches. They sat in the car, eating in silence while the rain battered the roof, both refusing to acknowledge the growing tension as they neared the institute. At five-thirty, she missed a call from John, swiftly followed by a flurry of concerned text messages that she chose to ignore.

There were more important things on her mind.

She gazed out her window at the rolling hills, their peaks obscured by low-hanging clouds. "I'm scared," she said suddenly, breaking twenty minutes of silence.

Larkin glanced at her, but offered no words of wisdom.

That was fine. Becky wasn't big on small talk. When Larkin had something to say, she was confident he would say it. For now, they would drive on, through the rain-lashed Highlands and beneath a sky pregnant with misery. An appointment with Quintin Horsham-Blake awaited, a man who was possibly the only person on Earth who knew what happened to her mother.

Apart from Tommy.

Indeed. Tommy would know. She had a feeling Tommy

knew everything. That Tommy was responsible. That Tommy had *taken* her mother.

And that now...

Becky shivered.

...he wanted *her*.

18

Gravel crackled beneath the tyres of Larkin's vehicle as they pulled into the Beechburn Institute car park shortly after seven. They were ridiculously late, the inclement conditions doubling the time of their journey, and the Institute's brief window of visiting hours had long since passed. But Larkin was a police officer, and Becky hoped that if anyone could talk their way into meeting the elusive Horsham-Blake, it was him.

The institute itself was a run-down affair. Isolated in a deep valley, it looked like a borstal, with tall brick walls encompassing a brutalist concrete monstrosity that could only have been dreamt-up in the sixties.

Before they left the car, Becky tapped out a message to John telling him she would be home tomorrow afternoon, and that she was with a police detective. She wrote she was safe, and that he needn't worry, then deleted the latter part of the message and hit send.

"Ready?" asked Larkin.

"Guess so," she said, placing her hand on the door release. "You know, my mum's been gone for forty years. I never thought I'd actually find out what happened to her, and I made peace with that. It took a long time." A chill ran through her body, and she gathered her thoughts while Larkin waited respectfully. "When I found these videos, it reopened old wounds. Suddenly, here was *Rumplejack,* and Tommy, and the murders... and now you've traced this man who might know what happened, and what's *currently* happening, and, I... I just..."

Larkin placed his hand on hers. "One week ago," he said, "if you'd asked me if I believed in ghosts or, I dunno, the supernatural or some shite, I'd have told you to piss off. Now, I've driven a one-time murder suspect halfway up the country to speak to a ninety-year-old loony about his haunted children's TV show." He patted her hand. "So don't worry. We're in this together."

"Thank you," she said, and stepped out into the drizzle, zipping up her coat. There were three cars parked outside, all of them in the STAFF ONLY section.

"Shall we?"

She turned to Larkin, who at least had the foresight to bring an umbrella. He held it above her, and she listened to the raindrops drumming off the fabric. She adored the sound of the rain, and scurried beneath the brolly, trying not to get too close to the detective and accidentally brush his arm. God, he really did resemble Jason Statham. Should she tell him?

No. Don't make it weird.

Together, they walked to the faded grey door. Larkin punched the buzzer. The speaker crackled, and he leaned closer. "This is Detective Constable Gregor Larkin. I spoke on the phone with—"

The speaker emitted a shrill whine, and Larkin pushed the door open. He glanced back at Becky with an expression she couldn't read, and held the door for her. Once inside, he shook off his brolly and left it by the entrance, as a middle-aged man in a white uniform ambled towards them.

"Good evening," said Larkin. Becky was pleased he was with her. There was no way she could have done this by herself. At best, she would have made the journey to the institute, stood outside for an hour, terrified to enter... and then gone home again. But if there was one thing cops excelled at — other than abusing their authority — it was talking.

"I'm Detective Constable Larkin," he said, flashing his badge. "Sorry we're so late, but—"

"He won't talk to you," the man in the white coat said. Was he a doctor? He didn't *look* like a doctor, with his scuffed shoes and threadbare trousers and hands that needed a damn good scrub. "He's not spoken in a long time."

"Aye, well, regardless—"

"And he requested no visitors," the doctor said.

"I thought he didn't speak?"

"Oh, he speaks, but rarely. When he checked himself in, Mr Horsham-Blake asked us to honour several requests." The doctor sounded utterly disinterested. "No visitors and no television, among others. That's why he's in solitary. Been there for forty years. If he was mad *before,* well..."

"He's been in solitary for forty fucking years?" said Larkin.

"As per another of his requests, yes. Mr Horsham-Blake is a very private individual. But—" the doctor thrust a ring-binder at Larkin — "all the information you require is contained in these files." He glanced past them, staring down a corridor. "That way," he said, pointing. "First left, second right, third door on the left."

"You won't be accompanying us?"

"Heavens, no," the man said. "I've an institute to run."

"Aye, seems busy," said Larkin, glancing across the empty reception area. "Will someone be there to let us in?"

"Certainly. Mr Horsham-Blake will decide if he'd like to discuss matters with you."

Larkin sighed impatiently. "No. I mean, is there a member of staff with the key to his cell?"

That made the doctor giggle. It was a curious sound. "Oh, we don't have a key, Detective. Mr Horsham-Blake does. *He* has the only key." The doctor smiled. "Another one of his amusing little requests. Should you require access, only he may grant it."

"What the fuck are you talking about?" Larkin growled. "You agreed to this?"

"My superior did, yes. Mr Horsham-Blake was a wealthy man, Detective. He pays well for his stay here, and we look after him according to his needs. We care about our patients, Detective. Despite what you may have read in the gutter press, we care very much."

With that, the doctor turned and left. Becky looked around, but found no other staff. No receptionist, no orderlies, no janitors... nobody.

"Fucking nutter," said Larkin. "You catch those directions?"

"First left, second right, third door on the left," she said.

"Good memory."

She smiled, neglecting to mention she had been chanting the words in her head since the moment she heard them.

Larkin faced down the corridor. It was lined with doors, some of them open, some of them closed. "You ever see *The Silence of the Lambs?*"

"I wish you hadn't reminded me of that," she said, and Larkin placed a hand on the small of her back and gently urged her forwards.

"Come on, let's get this over with."

∽

They stood before the door in the corridor's deafening silence.

The place was deserted, and after some of the real-life horror stories Becky had read about the institute online, she wasn't surprised.

"Guess we knock," she said, hugging her arms around her chest as a shiver passed through her.

"Unorthodox," said Larkin. "But what the hell." He rapped his knuckles against the metal door. "Mr Horsham-Blake? This is Detective Constable Larkin. I need to talk to you." He waited. "It's urgent."

Then someone spoke. An old voice, frail and cracked as if it had gone unused for decades.

"Thank you for your interest, but I am not accepting visitors at this time. Please do not call again."

Larkin glanced at Becky. "It's about *Rumplejack*. It's about Rotten Tommy."

A moment's silence, then the fluttering of soft laughter. *"Well, there's a name I hoped I'd never hear again. Thank you, detective, for reminding an old man of his greatest terror. Now, kindly leave and do not return until I am dead and happily in my grave. Good day."*

"Listen, you bastard, he's after *me* now. You understand?" Larkin banged on the door. "Blake! Are you there? Are you listening? You better be, because we're not going anywhere until—"

"We, detective? I was under the impression from your selfish words that you were quite alone."

Becky clenched her fists and moved closer to the door. "Hello, Mr Horsham-Blake. My name is Rebecca. You... you knew my mum."

"I knew a lot of people's mothers, darling. Most of them, I imagine, are dead now."

"Her name was Meredith. Meredith Tremayne. You did know her, didn't you?"

The man said nothing. Becky listened to shuffling steps on the other side of the door, and then a key was inserted into the lock.

"I think perhaps you'd better come inside, Rebecca Tremayne," he said, as the door swung open. "I imagine you're swiftly running out of time."

19

"So she's really gone?" asked Flora.

John nodded. "Seems that way. She's fucked off with some policeman to god-knows-where."

"And you believe her?"

He flopped down on the settee. "Where else could she go? A *friend's* house?"

Flora laughed at that, then felt bad. This was not funny. They had arrived at John and Becky's together, to talk to her sister, to explain themselves and figure out what came next. But Becky had not been home.

"That's so dangerous," she said. "She's alone with a cop and nobody knows where she is. Does she not *read* the news?"

"I've never seen *you* read a newspaper," said John.

"A newspaper? Okay, grandpa, I'll stick to getting my news from Facebook. Anyway, shut up. Aren't you worried about her?"

"Nope. You know what she's like. She'll have fluttered her eyelids at some old policeman and hoodwinked him into believing her stories. He's probably humouring her so he can get into her knickers." John rose, grunting as he did so. "Gonna get a beer. Want anything?"

"Gin and coke."

As John retrieved their drinks, Flora's gaze wandered to the wall of photographs. Taking pride of place in the centre was a snap of John and Becky's wedding day. The pair looked so happy, John grinning behind a beard he hadn't sported for years, Becky beaming in a vintage wedding dress she had bought secondhand.

Dammit, what they were doing was wrong. Sure, she had never been close with her sister, but they were still family. She averted her eyes, turning to the TV, where a video recorder sat on the carpet, attached to the screen by a host of chunky wires.

"So, you wanna fuck?" John asked as he entered, handing her an ice cold glass of gin.

"What?"

"This is a rare opportunity, babes. How often does Becky go out overnight? We've got the whole place to ourselves!"

"Later." She gestured towards the TV. "These videos she's obsessed with. Have you seen them?"

John took a long drink. "She showed me a minute or so. It was boring. Some stupid kids show. She's always watching crap like that. Your mum was in a lot of shite. Oh, uh, no offence," he added.

"Some taken, but whatever. Let's watch one."

"You sure? There's a bed upstairs that hasn't seen any action for months, and my dick is—"

"Come on, just a few minutes. It'd be nice to see my mum again."

John smiled at her. "Shit, sorry. Okay, put it on. But afterwards…"

"After," said Flora, "I'm all yours."

∽

Becky entered the room, Larkin right behind her. It was dark, pitch black, and she found the switch.

"Mind if I put the light on?"

"Go ahead," Horsham-Blake replied. "I wouldn't have noticed anyway."

Becky flipped the switch, half-closing her eyes as a harsh fluorescent bulb burst into life, revealing padded white walls and a malnourished man perched on the edge of a bed. His skin — which presumably hadn't seen daylight in decades — was so gossamer-thin that it had become translucent, like a skull wrapped in cobwebs. He didn't look up as they entered, for he had no eyes. Where once they had sat were now two empty sockets set deep into his withered face.

"I'd offer you a seat, or a drink," the man said. "But I have neither. Oh, and please close and lock the door behind you."

Larkin did so.

"Keep the door locked night and day," said Horsham-Blake.

"So Tommy can't come out to play," finished Larkin.

"That's correct," the old man smiled. "Terribly sorry to hear you're going to die."

"Excuse me?"

"Death. The end. The shuffling off from this mortal coil. It's coming for you, dear boy. If you know the song, then you are, as they used to say, royally *fucked*. I presume you've seen him already, hmm? Our old friend Tommy?"

"We've met, yeah."

"He's rotten, isn't he? Rotten Tommy, that's what we used to call him on set. You could smell him from a mile off.

Rotten Tommy. Ro-o-o-o-o-tten Tommy. Rotten, rotten, rotten. Mr Rotten Tom—"

"What do you know about him?" interrupted Larkin.

"What would you *like* to know?"

"How about who is he, and what does he want?"

"My dad called him a devil," Becky interjected. "A demon."

"Oh, he's no demon. Just a very unpleasant boy who has, I imagine, grown into a very unpleasant man."

"That's putting it mildly," said Larkin. "He's killed two people already."

"Only two?" Horsham-Blake laughed. "My word, he's only getting started! Much more blood will be spilled before Tommy finds what he's looking for."

"And what *is* he looking for?" asked Becky.

"Oh, I don't know. A friend, perchance. You should ask your mother."

"My mum's been missing for forty years."

"Oh, I doubt that. You wouldn't be here if you hadn't found her."

Riddles. He was talking in riddles. Becky wanted to grab him, to *shake* him, to demand answers. But she worried that if she did, she would kill the fragile creature. It looked like a gust of wind would wrench the pale skin from his meagre bones.

"I haven't found her," she said. "I found some videotapes with—"

"Yes, precisely. You found *Rumplejack*. Otherwise, Tommy would never have found *you*. It seems the intervening years have failed to erode his inexhaustible patience. Of course, I *had* hoped the tapes would remain lost until *after* I was dead, but such is the felicitous nature of fate. I expect he'll come for me next. This door won't hold him. In a way, you've doomed me, the pair of you. Isn't that quaint? You came seeking answers to save your souls, and you've inadvertently cost me my own. Well, you have to laugh, I suppose."

"You're insane," said Larkin with a shake of his head.

"We *are* in a mental institute, you impertinent clod. What *did* you expect?"

"What about my mum?" Becky asked. "And what about *Rumplejack?* What *was* that show?"

"Oh, it was innocent enough, at first. A children's series using puppets to teach basic life lessons. The usual claptrap. I thought I was above it, but I owed a friend a favour, and I've never been one to turn down money. Everything was going fine, until we started putting the episodes together. That's when we realised the show was editing itself, incorporating footage we hadn't shot. Say, do either of you have a cigarette? I haven't had a smoke since 1984."

"Mine are in the car," said Becky.

"Shame. It would have been nice. Anyway, what was I saying? Oh yes, *Rumplejack*. The sort of foolish name only a writer could concoct. We didn't know it was a real place. I suppose it wasn't, not until filming commenced."

"What are you *talking* about? I don't understand."

"Nobody understood at the time, either. Only your mother seemed to. Like I said, ask her."

Becky closed her eyes, a stress-induced headache building. She was getting angry. Angry and frustrated and upset. "I already told you," she said through gritted teeth. "She's been missing for forty years."

"Until you found her."

"I haven't fucking found her!"

The man pounded a fist against his thigh, producing a

plume of dust. "You found the tapes! You know where she is. She's in Rumplejack!"

"That's just a TV show!"

The man leaned back, his bones clicking as he did so. "No, it's real, and doubtlessly still standing. I imagine your mother still lives there. Nobody ever *leaves* Rumplejack. Not even me."

"I've heard enough of this bollocks," said Larkin. "I can see this was a waste of time."

Horsham-Blake pulled an amused face. "So be it. Enjoy your death, lawman. As for you, Rebecca Tremayne, daughter of Meredith. Soon, you will *wish* you were dead. I wish I was. But it's gone too far, don't you think? I can't give up now, not after... how long did you say it's been?"

"Forty years," said Becky.

Larkin unlocked the cell. "You coming?"

"In a minute," she said, letting the detective storm out.

"Forty years," said Horsham-Blake, flinching as the door slammed shut. "Please, give me your hand." He held out an emaciated claw with untrimmed nails that hooked like talons. Despite her natural aversion to physical contact, Becky took it in her own.

"Forty years," the man repeated. "If your mother's been with him that long, prepare yourself. She won't be the same. None of them will. The cast, the crew... those that weren't murdered outright will all still be there. There's no escape from Rumplejack... just like there's no escape from Rotten Tommy."

She leaned in closer. "How do I get there?"

"Your friend will die."

"What about me?"

"Oh, *you* won't die. It's you he wants. It's you he's *always* wanted. I only hope that if he finds you, perhaps he'll finally leave me alone. Then, I can die an old, but very happy, man."

"So tell me how to get there."

"Do you have a pen? You'll want to write this down." He smiled to himself as she rummaged in her bag for a notepad, then gave her the directions.

"Is there anything else you can tell me?" she asked.

"No. I'm sorry. I wish I could help." He reached for his face and scratched inside one of his eye sockets. "It was nice meeting you, Rebecca Tremayne, but I'm tired now." He lay back across his bed. "Close the door on your way out. And please, if you see your mother... do pass on my regards."

20

"My name's S*tick'emup*," said the man in the horse costume to the man in the bear suit. *"And I say... stick 'em up, Silly Bear!"*

"What the fuck is this shit?" asked John. "There aren't enough beers in the fridge to get me through another ten minutes of this. Hell, there aren't enough beers in the world."

"It's... not great," agreed Flora, though she struggled to rip her eyes from the childish nonsense unfolding on the screen.

They were twenty minutes into the show, thanks to some judicious fast-forwarding past the interminable opening scene with the burnt woman and the lighthouse. Now the 'action' had moved to a police station, or the *jailhouse* as the horse in the jeans and stetson called it.

"Shouldn't the cowboy be a cow?" John mused. "I mean, the clue's in the name." He swallowed the last dregs of his beer and placed the empty bottle on the side table. "Are we done? That bear is giving me flashbacks to Bungle from *Rainbow*."

"I thought Becky said mum was in this. I've not seen her."

"From what I saw, she had a two-second cameo as a prisoner, and we've got three full hours of this garbage. She could be anywhere on the tape." He gave Flora a squeeze. "Come on, let's go to bed."

"It's not even eight."

John grinned. "I didn't mean to sleep."

"I just want to watch until she's on, okay? It shouldn't be long." She knew she had to be careful. If John started sulking, the night would be ruined. But couldn't he keep his monster cock in his pants for a few more minutes?

"Hey," he said. "Look at that."

She glanced at the screen. The camera prowled along a quiet city street. It was night, and the streetlamps glowed hazily.

"What is it? Did you see my mum?"

"No." His voice was unusually distracted. "That's outside."

"Well done, John. You've learnt the difference between inside and outside. Have a sticker."

"No, I mean that's the street around the corner. See? There's Becky's favourite Chinese restaurant. Y'know, the one she orders a lemon chicken from every Thursday."

"Shit, you're right." Flora chuckled. "Didn't realise it'd been around so long."

"It hasn't," said John. "It opened about, I dunno, ten years ago."

"So what's it doing on a tape that's been buried in a wall for forty years?"

John didn't have an answer for that.

Neither of them did.

The camera continued down the street, but not with the

smooth, gliding motion of modern movies and TV shows. The handheld picture jerked with each step, reminding Flora of *The Blair Witch Project,* a film that had made her nauseous on her one and only viewing.

The unseen cameraman turned the corner.

"Look," said John. "You can see our house!"

"Yeah," smiled Flora, though she found the idea more sinister than charming. "You're right. Let's switch this off and go to bed."

"Wait a minute, it's getting good!"

She reached for his crotch, gripping his cock through his jeans. "Come on, turn it off."

"What, are you scared?" He snorted in derision. "Watch, he's almost at the gate. Reckon your dad's filming?"

"Must be."

The cameraman arrived at the house. A hand appeared, thick and white like soft dough, and pushed the gate open.

"Was your dad the fucking Marshmallow Man?" laughed John.

"Switch it off, John. Please."

"What? Calm down!"

"John, look at the door. It's red, John. It's fucking *red.*"

"So?"

"So you painted it red last summer."

"Oh," he said. He screwed up his face in concentration. "Wait, did Becky film this?"

The camera operator trudged up the gravel path.

"John, I don't like this."

"Oh, fucking relax. It's an old home movie."

But it wasn't old. The restaurant, the door... even the cars on the street were modern. This had been filmed in the last few days, Flora was sure of it. It must have been Becky. No one else could—

The white hand crossed into the frame again, the fingers splaying as they pressed against the door. Without thinking, Flora glanced at the hallway. From her vantage point on the settee, she couldn't see the front door. She wanted to ask John to check, but he'd only laugh at her.

On the TV screen, the camera turned away, heading down the paved track along the side of the house towards the back garden.

Could it be Becky? Could they somehow be watching a live recording of her sister trying to catch them in the act?

"Pause it," she said. When John didn't react, she snatched the controller from his hand and hit PAUSE. The image stopped. She let out a sigh, and started to laugh. "Shit, I thought I was going crazy there. Sorry." She unpaused the tape and snuggled into John's arm, smiling at the idea of Becky lurking around outside with a camcorder, dressed head to toe in camouflage gear in an attempt to film them *in flagrante delicto*. Her smile broadened at her use of Latin.

See, Becky? I can be smart like you when I want.

Then she looked at the screen, and there, *there* she was, her and John together, sitting exactly as they were now, the camera peering in.

"John," said Flora. "That's us."

It was the most blatantly obvious thing she'd ever said, but what else *could* she say? She wanted to turn to the window, to catch the voyeur, but she was too afraid. They had *paused* the video a few seconds ago.

John leapt on his feet. "Alright, who's there?" he demanded.

"John, wait!"

She watched him from the settee, frozen in place. He stood by the window, gazing out. If anyone was there, he would surely have seen them. He looked left, then right, then left again. When he turned back to her, his face was blank.

"No one there," he said, and forced a warped smile. "Weird."

His expression changed. Flora watched it happen, his face falling, eyes widening in terror. He swallowed loudly. "Flora, listen to me very carefully."

"What? What's wrong?"

He was looking at something. The television.

She followed his gaze.

"Don't look at—" he started to say, but he was too late.

She was on TV.

Flora saw herself on the settee, an enormous man in black standing behind her, his arm raised. Her stomach dropped, and she screamed and threw herself forwards, tripping over the coffee table and sprawling across the floor, scrambling to safety.

When she turned back, no one was there. John raced for the video and ejected the tape, yanking it from the recorder like a rotten tooth from a diseased gum. He hurled it at the wall, where it smacked against the paint and clattered to the floor, unbroken.

Flora stared at him from her low vantage point on the floor. When she tried to speak, all that came out was a sob.

"What just happened?" asked John, as she started to cry. "What the *fuck* just happened?"

21

"There's a Bed and Breakfast up ahead," said Larkin as he navigated the winding country roads, the trees flashing by like fleeting ghosts caught in the headlights. "Guess we should stop for the night."

"Yeah," said Becky. "According to the directions, Rumplejack is a good couple of hours away, depending on the weather. I don't know about you, but I'd rather arrive in daylight."

She yawned. God, she was tired. The busy day had depleted her social battery, and when she tried to relax in the car, Horsham-Blake's words repeated in her head until they no longer made any sense.

I only hope that if he finds you, perhaps he'll finally leave me alone.

After a while, she had given in and let the calming *whick whick* of the windscreen wipers lull her into a trance.

They took a turn at a sign advertising Gracie's B&B, and drove down a flooded track, guided by the welcoming lights of a distant farmhouse. She wondered what John was up to. Was he with Flora? She hadn't given the matter much thought. Her personal relationships were of secondary importance to finding the truth about Rumplejack... and about her mother. Forty years of waiting, of wondering. And now, it was drawing to a close. For the first time in decades, she felt a trace of hope that her mum could still, somehow, be alive. All she was going on was the word of an asylum inmate, but that was better than nothing. And hell, the line between sane and insane was dreadfully thin. It was a numbers game. The only reason some were judged to be crazy was because there were more 'normal' people out there. Should the balance ever shift, the supposedly normal folk would become the pariahs.

The car rolled to a stop, and Larkin walked to the farmhouse to book two adjacent rooms while Becky waited in the vehicle. On his signal, she grabbed her rucksack and met him in the doorway.

"You sure you'll be okay on your own?" he asked, as they trudged up the stairs to their rooms.

"I'm looking forward to it."

"Ouch," he winced.

Wait. She had said something wrong, though she wasn't sure what. She considered her words. It was true, she *was* looking forward to some alone time... but she realised now he thought she meant away from him *specifically*. She hurriedly corrected herself. "It's nothing personal. I need some space to gather my thoughts, that's all. I'm glad you're here. If I was alone, things would be... a lot slower."

He smiled. "Good. Because I'm glad *you're* here. I don't know anyone else who'd believe me."

He looked at her, and she thought he was going to kiss her.

"Well, good night," she said.

"Aye, night." He made to leave, then stopped. "It's still pretty early. Care for a nightcap?"

"I wouldn't be great company tonight," she said, though part of her wanted to. "Plus, I have to phone my husband."

"Of course. Well, you know where I am if you need me."

"Right in there," she said, pointing at his door. She gave him a thumbs up.

What are you doing?

"Okay," she said. "Good night."

"You already said that."

"Yes I did," she said, adopting a dreadful Texan accent for some inexplicable reason. She started to say something else — *toodle pip* was on the tip of her tongue — before she changed her mind and turned away, entering her room and closing the door behind her. There, she leaned against it and inhaled deeply, letting the inevitable exhalation relax her tense body.

"Toodle pip," she muttered, raising her eyebrows. "Close one."

The room was small but cosy, and she sat on the bed and took two paracetamol and two ibuprofen for her headache. This was the most socialising she had accomplished in one day for years, and while she enjoyed Larkin's company — especially the way he was unafraid to sit in silence — the exertion had wiped her out.

She placed her bag on the duvet and carefully removed her belongings, laying out her deodorant and phone and contact lens case and hairbrush in the precise way they sat on her bedside cabinet at home. In this unfamiliar environment, even the smallest nod to her routine was a welcome comfort. Her phone displayed no new messages, which was a damning indictment of both her lack of adult friendships and her husband's attitude towards her.

"I tell him I've run off with a strange man, and he just fucking accepts it."

She changed into pyjamas patterned with cartoon ducks, and placed Grumpus the penguin on her pillow, running his flipper through her fingers. Rain spattered against the window, and she curled up with Grumpus and listened, thinking about how the detective had invited her in for a drink. Did he expect her to go to bed with him? She couldn't tell. It might have been fun, she had to admit. Something to take her mind off, well... *everything* else. It was the closest she would ever get to sleeping with Jason Statham, that was for sure.

And, lest you forget, your husband is *having an affair.*

The more she thought about it, the more obvious it seemed. The late nights, the weekends away, the constant messaging. Christ, he had made a buffoon out of her. And as for Flora...

The pair were equally guilty, both parties complicit in the cruelest kind of subterfuge. When she had phoned earlier, excited and frightened by the video, they had been having sex, hadn't they? Both of them, in bed, carrying on while she was on the phone. They probably laughed about it afterwards, lying there, naked and soaked in each other's revolting juices.

She thought about Larkin. Should she do it? Did he even want to? Fuck, why did she have to overthink every fucking last little thing?

"Fuck's sake," she said. Tired she may have been, but she was not falling asleep any time soon. Sometimes — more often than she cared to admit — she wished she could switch her mind into rest mode. Just long enough to allow her to fall asleep. Was that too much to ask?

She checked her phone again. No messages. She would

call John. Give him a chance to explain, to apologise, to beg for forgiveness. Then she would end it. He *deserved* no forgiveness. Her husband was rotten.

Rotten...

Rotten to the core. She snatched up her phone and prepared to call him, staring at the contacts screen, at his name, at the small photo of his smiling face. From before. From happier times. When he still loved her and cared for her.

Listening to the pitter patter of the rain, she stared at the photo and wondered if he was thinking of her.

~

"Oh God, Flora, you bitch!" John cried. "I'm gonna come! I'm gonna..."

And then John did, as promised, ejaculate into his wife's sister's vagina. Panting, he slid out of her and rolled onto his back. The sex had been good, but not great. Something was off with Flora. She had hardly said a word throughout, which was unlike her. He figured she was dwelling on the strange video, whereas he had used the sex to banish it from his mind.

A shared hallucination. It had to have been. Becky had planted the seed in both their minds that the videos were somehow malicious, and they had unwittingly worked themselves into a frenzy. He placed his hand on the curve of Flora's bare arse. "Hey babe, you okay?"

"I'm fine."

"You wanna go again in a minute?"

She shifted her position to sidle away from his touch. "Not tonight."

Fucking Becky. Their first full night alone together, and

somehow his wife had ruined it without even being present. Her and her stupid fucking videos. Annoyed, he tucked his feet into his slippers and dressed in his robe. If he wasn't going to get any more loving from Flora, and he wasn't going to get any sleep, he may as well go downstairs and get a fucking drink. One beer remained in the fridge, and he cracked it open and trudged back up to the spare room, his current home office until the workmen completed the extension. There, he opened Facebook and scrolled mindlessly as he sipped on his drink.

His aunt Geraldine was complaining about immigrants, while Peter from work had posted photos from his holiday in Tenerife, including several snaps of Peter's young wife in a green thong bikini.

"Nice," said John.

He heard a noise from the adjacent room and looked up from his phone. It sounded like a window opening, and he ignored it. Flora was either too warm or making a bid for freedom, and he figured the first option was most likely, as there were a perfectly good set of stairs leading down to the front door if she wished to leave.

"John?"

Her voice drifted through the wall. Hey, maybe she was horny after all? John glanced at the photos of Peter's wife to get himself in the mood, opening his gown to air his cock and balls before heading back to—

"John, is that you?"

A tremor, starting in his fingertips, snaked its way through his limbs.

"John...?"

A scream. Suddenly his skin felt too tight.

"Flora," he said, his voice like the dry snap of a branch. He lumbered forwards and stepped into the upper hallway, leaning one hand on the wall. What the fuck was going on, what the fuck was *happening?* He hesitated before the bedroom door, considering whether to call her name.

Then Flora screamed again, and John nudged the door open with a trembling hand. The hallway light spilled into the room, the grisly tableaux revealing itself like a waking nightmare.

Flora was on her knees, naked and screaming, her arms outstretched and reaching for John, desperate fingers clawing at thin air. Behind her stood the man from the video, his feet firmly planted on her ankles. The brute was hunched over, and his bone-white hands gripped Flora's hair, stretching her taut.

A new sound assaulted John's ears, the grinding crunch of Flora's ankle bones under the immense weight of the man's boots. John looked at her, and as thick clumps of Flora's hair came away in the man's hand, along with much of her scalp, he could do nothing but scream. Blood spilled down Flora's wretched, screaming face as the man peeled the top of her head back, exposing the slick sheen of a vein-threaded skull. Her body slumped, but the killer was apparently just getting started.

The man clasped her head between his monstrous hands, hooking several fingers into her open mouth and snapping her back into an upright position. Crimson rivulets of blood cascaded over her breasts, her body a trembling, naked horror.

Shaking free of his lethargy, John stepped back, his survival instincts kicking in. Could the man see him? Were those cavernous black pits on his face really *eyes?* Was that spiralling cavity a mouth?

The skin on Flora's neck stretched, and as John retreated to the bedroom door, splits appeared along her jugular. Tiny pin-prick holes at first, from which thin streams of blood oozed like burst acne, and as the holes widened, her neck elongated, *distorted,* the fragile skin tearing and exposing dense muscle.

The muscle tore. John heard it before he saw it, the head detaching from the body, forced apart with inhuman strength. Skin ruptured, veins and arteries snapping and spraying madly across the room, coating the walls, the bed, and the man's long, dark jacket. Flora's arms dropped to her sides. There was a gap of around an inch between her neck and her shoulders, her spinal column visible between them. The big man yanked her cranium back and forth, the vertebrae grinding under the pressure until — with one final eruption of violence — he wrenched her head from her body.

Flora's lifeless torso splatted onto the ground, blood pumping from the ragged stump between her shoulders. The pool spread across the floor like an infectious disease, and John stepped away as it neared his slippers. When he looked up, the man was holding Flora's decapitated head. It dropped from his fingers with a dull *thud.*

He was looking at John.

There was no doubt about it.

The man was staring directly at him.

22

With his gown flapping behind him, John ran from the room, his meaty cock slapping rhythmically against his thighs. The image of Flora's severed head, open-mouthed and horrified, was imprinted on his retinas, and would remain there until the day he died. Which, if he didn't hurry, would be today. He raced down the stairs, afraid to check if the man was following. The front door was within reach. Unable to slow himself in time, he smacked into the door and turned the handle.

It was locked.

"The keys," he said, as he realised they were lying upstairs by the bed in his crumpled jeans. What about the back door? They lived in a safe neighbourhood, and usually left it unlocked... but not tonight. John had secured the door in case Becky decided to come home early and surprise them. Dammit, the bitch spoiled everything!

Thunderous footsteps rattled the building. The man was coming for him.

John looked around for ideas. Could he escape through a window? No, they were triple-glazed, and didn't open wide enough for him to squeeze through. What about the police? Yes! His phone was still in the pocket of his gown. He could call the cops, if he only had a quiet place to hide.

His gaze settled on the cupboard beneath the stairs, and he ran to it, dropping to his knees and pulling the hidden door open. The space was packed with cardboard boxes, but he scrambled in, curling into a ball to squeeze alongside the vacuum cleaner. Barely able to move, he stretched for the door. It was not designed to be closed from the inside, but using the tips of his fingers, he managed to get it mostly shut.

Monotonous footsteps resounded directly above him as the man descended the stairs. Tucked into the cramped space, John manoeuvred his arm, groping for the phone in his pocket. The footsteps paused momentarily as the man reached the bottom of the stairs. He was close.

Cautiously, John unlocked his phone, the bright light illuminating the restrictive confines of the cupboard. What to do? He couldn't call for help, not right now.

Can you text the police, he typed into Google, and clicked on the first result.

The footsteps resumed, drawing nearer. They stopped right outside the cupboard.

John's mind raced. With only a thin wooden door between him and the psychopath who had murdered his lover, he tried to concentrate on the phone. The screen shook mightily in his hand, adrenaline electrifying him like he'd just snorted the finest Colombian cocaine off a virgin's tits.

The webpage loaded, blighted by adverts and pop-ups. He closed them with quivering fingers, and the privacy statement appeared, asking if he accepted cookies.

Yes, I fucking accept them, he wanted to scream.

But he didn't. Instead, he scanned the information. Apparently, the public *could* text the police…

Yes, yes, yes!

…but only if their phone was pre-registered with the service.

Fuck, fuck, fuck!

Already his limbs were cramping. He could smell the man through the door. A foul odour, like rotten eggs.

More footsteps. The man was walking away. The living room door creaked open, then a few minutes later his boots clomped noisily on the kitchen's laminate flooring. Pain wracked John's legs. He wanted so badly to yell, to burst from this tiny space and stretch.

His phone pinged.

An Instagram notification appeared, and, in fright, the phone fell from his hand. It bounced on a cardboard box and dropped inside.

The footsteps returned, faster than before, pausing in the hallway. John froze. Fucking notifications. What if another came through? Dammit to hell! He waited, his eyes wet with tears, positive that at any moment, the door would fly off the hinges and two hands would drag him to his doom.

After what felt like an ice-age, the man moved again. He stomped past the cupboard, and John allowed himself a manic smile in the darkness. Okay, the bastard was leaving. Thank Christ. He would wait a while — as long as it took — until he was *sure* the intruder had left, and then—

His phone rang.

The intense brass instrumentation of *Goldfinger* blared from the speaker, the walls of the cardboard box somehow amplifying the volume.

"No!" whimpered John, squirming his body to reach the

phone. Shirley Bassey's voice belted out the titular word, and then the cupboard door *did* fly open, just as he had feared it would.

The big man grabbed him, hauling him from his hiding place by his numb, useless legs. John slid out, his bare arse scraping along the floor, and stared up into the hideously misshapen visage of Flora's killer.

"Please," he sobbed, raising his voice to be heard over the song. "I have money. Lots of money. You can have it all!"

He stared into the man's open mouth, half-expecting a funnel-web spider to emerge from the drooping coil. Instead, his head angled downwards to look at John's penis. He reached for it, prodding the flaccid member like an entomologist inspecting a rare find.

What was happening? Should he offer his body to the man? Was *that* what he wanted?

Too late, he discovered it was not. The enormous hand closed over his penis and testicles, squashing them in a vice-like grip. The man rose to his full stature and dragged John's limp body towards the staircase by his cock and balls. The pressure was unbearable, a searing, white-hot agony in his groin.

"Please! *Stop!*"

John felt his skin stretching. God, he actually felt it *stretching*. Only his head and shoulders touched the ground, the rest of him raised up, his legs bent at the knees.

"No, no!" he begged, as the man started up the stairs, using John's genitals like a suitcase handle. His head thudded off the first step, then the second, and halfway up, he heard the sound.

The harsh tearing.

His groin burned like it was aflame, and hot liquid gushed over his perineum and slithered into his arse crack.

He closed his eyes and tumbled down the stairs, smacking against each one before landing in a loose, sprawled heap. At first, he thought the man had released him. But when he noticed the rainbow of blood arcing from the mutilated area between his legs, and the nest of unkempt pubic hair surrounding the mess of shredded skin, he knew things had not gone well.

With his mind teetering on the brink of insanity, he looked up the stairs. The man had stopped, and pivoted to look at him. He opened his fist, inspecting the contents, and let a soggy, flattened appendage drop onto the step, blood seeping through his fingers.

"That's mine," John whimpered, as the big man started back down the stairs, reaching into his pocket and producing a bloodstained steel hammer.

John attempted to crawl away, but the pain was insurmountable. All he could do was shuffle back against the door and listen to Shirley Bassey crooning in the cupboard, as the man slowly descended.

The man who had butchered Flora.

The man who had destroyed his manhood.

The man who was about to kill him.

Yet none of that mattered, for all John could think about — as the big man loomed over him and brought the hammer screaming down onto his face — was, *what the hell is Shirley Bassey doing in the cupboard under the stairs?*

∼

Becky had waited long enough.

She quit the call and threw her phone onto the bed. If John wasn't going to answer — and she knew he could hear it, because he was one of those annoying pricks who *never* put his ringtone on silent, even at night — then fuck him.

"It's over, John," she said to the phone. "We're finished."

The idea scared her. The unknown, and the upending of long-held routines, shimmered on the horizon. God, how had it come to this? She had given him one last chance to explain himself, and the bastard didn't even have the balls to answer. Or maybe — and wasn't this a fine excuse — he was too busy screwing her sister?

In an act of defiance, she twisted her wedding and engagement rings around her finger to remove them. But the more she tried, the wider her fingers seemed to get, and the rings stuck on her knuckle. She went to the bathroom, running cold water over her hands and smearing soap over her finger, and tried again.

This time, she was successful.

"Fuck you!" she shouted, throwing the rings down and watching them rattle across the floor. "Fuck you, fuck you, fuck—"

The door flew open, slamming against the wall, and Becky whirled to see Larkin in the doorway.

"What's going on?" He looked around the room. "Is he here?"

Becky stared at him, mouth agape. Was he talking about John? How did he know?

Tommy. He's talking about Tommy.

That made more sense, but now she was unsure how to respond, standing like an idiot in her duck-print pyjamas, her hands red from the cold water, one finger slathered in soap.

"Everything is fine here," she said in her calmest voice. "Everything is ab-so-lute-ly perfect." She took a breath. "How... are you?"

"I'm... also fine," said Larkin. Unlike her, he looked good. Great, even, in his black trousers and tight white vest that clung to his aesthetically pleasing body. "Are you sure you're okay? You sounded, uh, perturbed."

Words deserted her. She saw him glance at her bed, where her plush penguin lay.

"That's Grumpus," she said. "He's not real, but he's still my best friend. I bring him everywhere, so if you're going to spend the night with me, he'll be there too, okay?"

Larkin looked at her with an expression she couldn't read, so, panicking, she continued to speak.

"And another thing. I'm autistic, okay? You might know that from the interview after my dad died, but if not, I'm telling you so you can't say you weren't aware. Apparently it's a problem for people, even if they liked me before. My husband, for example, who is cheating on me with my sister. No, wait, not my husband, my *ex*-husband, because we are through, one-hundred percent done, finished, finito. So if, y'know, that's a problem for you, tell me now so I can stop seducing you."

She still couldn't read Larkin's face. Should she keep talking?

The detective cleared his throat. "Are you... are you *seducing* me right now? Is that what's happening?"

"This is a seduction, yes," she said. "Would you like to sleep with me?"

He stared at her, saying nothing. What was he thinking?

"It's the duck pyjamas, isn't it?" she asked, unable to stop herself. "You think they're silly. I'll take them off. I mean, not right now, not if you don't want me to. But obviously, I'll take them off if we go to bed together. Not that I'm pressuring you or anything, I just thought that, with everything that's going on, we could die tomorrow, or even tonight, and I basically just got divorced, though he doesn't know it yet, and to be honest, I'm pretty scared about what we're going to find tomorrow if we look for Rumplejack, and—"

"Are you finished?"

Becky's heart pounded. She drew in a deep breath. "I think so, yeah. I could keep going, but I'd rather not, because I feel stupid enough. I'm sorry, I'm not good at this. I thought you were interested in me, which I guess was my first mistake, and then I thought I was capable of being seductive, but I can't seem to do that either." Her gaze dropped to the floor. "Okay. *Now* I'm finished." She paused. "I think."

Larkin took a step closer, shutting the door behind him. His face lit up with a smirk. "I think your seduction technique is great. Unconventional, aye, but that's not a bad thing." He was close enough for her to feel his breath on her face, and for once, she didn't mind. He kissed her; on the cheek at first, then on her lips.

She pulled back, somehow both embarrassed and aroused. "So you're telling me it worked?" She smiled as his hands slid down her back, investigating her cool, soft flesh. "I seduced you?"

"You did," said Larkin. "You seduced the *fuck* out of me."

They kissed again, and he pulled her closer. She felt his erection through his trousers.

"And you don't mind Grumpus the penguin?"

He squeezed her bum, and said, "I don't mind Grumpus."

She kissed his neck, running her hands over his biceps. He felt good and strong. He smelled nice, too. "And me being autistic doesn't bother you?"

"Of course not. I wouldn't change a thing about you."

"Not even my duck pyjamas?"

"Oh, now they *are* a problem," he said, his fingers finding the button of her pyjama top and undoing it. "These pyjamas are totally unacceptable." He worked the second button free, exposing her cleavage. "In fact, I'm afraid I'm going to have to ask you to remove them."

"Right now?" she smiled.

"Yeah. Don't forget, I'm a cop. I could arrest you."

"On what charge?" she asked, as he undid the remaining buttons and she shrugged her pyjama top to the floor. "Indecent exposure?"

"No." He placed his hands on her breasts. "For resisting my charms." He suddenly released her. "I'm sorry, I can't believe I said that."

"Wow," she laughed. *"Smooth."*

He looked away and scratched at his chin. "I'm, uh, also not very good at this."

She kissed him, her bare breasts pressing against his chest, and said, "Maybe we shouldn't talk at all?"

He nodded at that, and Becky let him lift and carry her to the bed, where he laid her down and removed his vest. She smiled to herself.

She had always appreciated a man with a muscular torso.

But more than that, she appreciated a man who knew when not to talk.

23

They left at sunrise.

The endless downpour raged on as they pulled out of the carpark, a scrap of paper containing Horsham-Blake's directions clutched in Becky's hands. They headed north, stopping only twice; once at a roadside service station for a bacon roll and a coffee to eat on the go, and once on the outskirts of Auchenmullan, where the road had been fenced off with signs proclaiming

NO ENTRY
PROPERTY OF THE RYLAK CORPORATION

The closure forced them to take a lengthy detour, but an hour later they pulled onto the coastal road, and the rugged, mountainous terrain faded into the rearview mirror. According to the directions, they were now within spitting distance of Rumplejack.

"I had a nice time last night," Larkin said. "With you, I mean."

"Yeah. Me too."

He accelerated, overtaking a tractor that was going no faster than twenty. "I know you've got some things to work out with your husband. But if we get through this... *when* we get through this, I'd like to see you again."

Becky pondered this information. Outside, a forest flashed by, the low sun strobing as it passed the treetops. She looked away, staring straight ahead at the undulating road. "I'd like that too. Though, like you say, things are messy at home, and they're only going to get worse for a while. I don't want to rush into anything."

"I can understand that. And I'm happy to wait." He snorted. "Fuck, I'll be happy to still be *alive.*"

She patted his thigh in a way she knew was supposed to comfort people, and they lapsed into an uneasy silence. She wondered if she would ever see John again, let alone divorce him. The idea that she could die today, and make his relationship with her sister that much easier, infuriated her. However, anger was preferable to fear, because while it gave her a headache, it didn't make her stomach hurt. She pulled Grumpus from her backpack and held him to her chest, secure in the knowledge that her penguin didn't bother Larkin.

They drove on, their progress constantly impeded by the flooded roads.

"Car's gonna be fucked after this," Larkin grumbled, as he slowly guided the vehicle through a trough of floodwater as high as the wheels. "Right, where now?"

"Follow the road," said Becky. "Should be a turnoff in the next few miles."

"What does it show you on the map?"

"Nothing." She hugged Grumpus. "What do we do if it's not there?"

"It'll be there. It has to be."

"Forty years have passed."

"Aye, but you saw the video. It was a whole town. There's no way they built that set. Even if the place has fallen into disrepair, some of those bloody lighthouses have been around for fucking decades."

"Centuries," she corrected. "The oldest manned lighthouse in Scotland was built in 1635 on the Isle of May, and it's still there, even though a new one replaced it in 1816. The engineer of *that* one was Robert Stevenson, who was responsible for lots of lighthouses, including my all-time favourite, the Bell Rock Lighthouse near Angus. That one's been standing for over two *hundred* years."

"Wow," said Larkin with a grin. "I've never met someone with a favourite lighthouse before. Or anyone who can *name* a lighthouse."

She shrugged, and glanced out the window. "They're a passion of mine."

"Why?"

Ah, the age old question. "They just are. I've had a few passions in my life, and most of them come and go, and occasionally come back again." She smiled to herself. "I've had obsessions with Egyptian mummies, which is quite common, and with the band Pulp, and with penguins and *Lord of the Rings* and frogs and *The Simpsons* and—" she hesitated, unable to look at him "—the actor Jason Statham. Basically, anything that isn't useful *at all*. But as for lighthouses... they'll forever be number one in my heart. I love them, and I always have, and I'm in my forties now, so chances are, I always will. I'd love to live in one." She smiled to herself. "Just me, all by myself, in my little lighthouse."

"You'd get bored," said Larkin. "Everyone needs company."

"Yeah, sure," she said, though she was lying. She knew

she wouldn't get bored. It was a dream of hers. Not just to live in the most perfectly designed buildings on the planet, but to be free of people. Alone, with no one to bother her. She had dreamt about it since childhood, and nowadays, to avoid an argument, whenever someone told her she'd get bored living on her own, she agreed with them. Life was too short to spend arguing with people.

"So, what's it like?" asked Larkin. He took a bend too sharply, the side wheels dipping into a ditch and spraying water over a bank of trees.

"What's what like?"

"Being autistic."

"I don't know," replied Becky. She had thought about it a lot over the last few years. "The thing is, it's all I've ever known. I was diagnosed at thirty-eight, and until then, I assumed everyone experienced life the same way I did; in a state of constant anxiety and confusion." She watched the windscreen wipers slide back and forth. "I didn't know I saw the world differently to some people."

"It's funny," said Larkin. "I thought it was just men. Don't think I've met an autistic woman before."

"Oh, you have. We're just better at hiding it. Masking, we call it. Women are taught from childhood to blend in. To smile and listen and not make a fuss about anything, or else we're seen as hard work. And whereas boys tend to obsess over things like trains, autistic girls might focus on more socially acceptable pursuits, like horses and ponies, and our games are all about having tea parties and running pretend shops. Basically, acclimatising to adult socialisation. As we get older, we get told we have anxiety or depression instead of being tested. Like in everything, there's a male bias, so women and girls slip through the cracks, living their lives in quiet confusion without ever knowing why." She leaned back in the seat. "Sorry for ranting, but that's just the—"

The car jolted to a stop, catapulting her forwards into her seatbelt.

"Ow!"

"Sorry," said Larkin sheepishly. "But... I think we're here."

The car rested on a single lane road that led up a hill, the track blocked by a tall, metal fence topped with coils of barbed wire. On the gate, a faded white sign read,

NO ENTRY
PROPERTY OF THE RYLAK CORPORATION

"We passed a sign like that a while ago," she said. "Outside that ghost town."

She got out of the car and walked to the fence, the rain drumming off her unprotected face. She moved to touch it—

"Wait," called Larkin, jogging to her side. "It could be electric."

"They'd have a warning." She placed her fingers on the hexagonal wires and peered through. Beyond, the North Sea roared in unending fury, the road winding down to the coast from the top of the hill.

Further down was a wooden sign. The elements had battered it into submission — the paint was faded, the wood black and rotten — but the words were still visible, words she was sure had been carved forty years ago by an underpaid intern on a Scottish TV show.

WELCOME TO RUMPLEJACK, the sign read.
YOU'RE NEVER FAR AWAY.

24

"It's real," said Becky, the howling gale whisking the words from her lips.

Larkin stood beside her, his hands in his pockets. "Why is it fenced off? What's the bloody Rylak Corporation?"

"I looked them up after the last sign. They're some research company. They seem to have buildings popping up around the country, but I couldn't find information on what they actually do."

"Never heard of them until today. I'll check once we get back to civilization."

Becky's gaze travelled up the gate. "So what now? Do we climb?"

"You see anyone watching? Any guards, or CCTV?"

They both looked, finding nothing but miles of fence stretching to the sea.

"We've not passed any buildings recently," said Larkin. "We're in the arse end of nowhere, and there's no one around." He shook the gate as if testing it, and turned to her. "Get in the car."

"Ohmygod," she whispered, looking from the car to the

gate and back again. A shiver ran down her spine. "You're going to do it, aren't you?"

"Damn right I am."

Visions of Jason Statham behind the wheel in *Death Race* flashed through her mind, followed by a cinematic image of the car bursting through the gate to Rumplejack, captured in slow motion and from multiple angles while an explosion went off for no reason behind them.

"You're really going to do it." She stared at him in admiration and... yes, *desire*. "You're going to *Statham* it."

"I'm going to what?"

"Statham it." He didn't seem to understand. "You're going to drive through the gate and knock it down. You're going to Statham us right through it."

His lips curled into a smile. "Ehh, no. I have a toolbox in the car. I'll find something in there to break the lock."

"Oh." Was he joking? "So why did you tell me to get in the car?"

"Because it's raining," he said. "You're getting wet."

Dejected, she climbed back into the vehicle, sitting alone with her action movie fantasies while Detective Constable Larkin, a man who could be Jason Statham's long-lost twin, rummaged around in the boot instead of slamming the accelerator and ploughing the vehicle through the fence. "Getting wet?" she grumbled, and looked out to sea. "You have no fucking idea."

∼

The chunky padlock offered some resistance, but with no one nearby to see or hear, Larkin quickly smashed it free with a wrench. The metal clunked to the ground, and he kicked it out of the way in miniature triumph.

Becky watched the detective through the blurry, rain-streaked windscreen. She didn't blame him for wanting an alternative to crashing through the gate. It wouldn't be good for his car. But still... it would have been so cool. A little excitement to offset the gnawing apprehension in her gut that felt like a rat chewing its way through the lining of her stomach.

If Rumplejack existed — if it was indeed a real place — then it was close. Would her mother be there? Would Tommy?

If your mother's been with him that long, prepare yourself, Horsham-Blake had said. *She won't be the same.*

Larkin entered the car and closed the door. "You ready?"

"No," she answered honestly. "But I'll never be ready, so let's go before I have a panic attack."

He pressed the accelerator, and they drove slowly through the open gate. As they crossed the manmade border, the sky cleared. Grey clouds dispersed as if evaporating, the rain halting for the first time in days. Becky lowered the sun visor as incandescent rays flared majestically off the calm sea that seconds before had raged in fury.

"That's not normal," she said. "Even in Scotland."

Larkin grunted in agreement, and as they crested the hill and began their descent, it appeared before them, shimmering in the impossible sunshine.

Rumplejack.

At last, the town's existence was beyond question.

A row of brightly coloured cottages sparkled in the sun, nestled beside the harbour and pier.

"It's pretty," said Becky.

"And bigger than I thought," said Larkin.

He wasn't wrong. The buildings stretched halfway up the hill. A church spire poked out from between a cluster of trees, surrounded by a cemetery, and along the beach from the harbour, she saw a funfair with a small rollercoaster and a half-size Ferris wheel. Far beyond that, a trail led to a rocky outcrop, upon which stood a glorious, sun-bleached lighthouse.

Keep the door locked night and day.

"There's no way this wouldn't be visible on Google Maps," said Larkin.

They approached the town limits, where a sign proclaimed

RUMPLEJACK
POP. 29

The twenty-nine had been scored through, with an ever-decreasing series of numbers scrawled on the sign, ending at sixteen.

Larkin slowed the car, then came to a complete stop, letting the engine idle. "Is this a bad idea?"

"Yup. You got a better one? If not, then keep driving."

He waited, perhaps for her to change her mind, then resumed the journey. The vehicle cruised into town and down the empty main street, passing a gift shop, a cafe, a chippy, and a charity shop. All appeared to be open for business.

"Let's get out and take a look," said Becky. "Park the car."

"Shouldn't be a problem. There are plenty of spaces."

It was true. There were no other vehicles. Even the harbour was missing the one thing harbours generally required; boats. On the drive down the hill, she had seen tall, white masts glinting in the sunlight. But now, she noticed they were all wrecks, the great wooden carcasses strewn across the beach like corpses on a battlefield.

Larkin killed the engine, and they exited. A light breeze ruffled Becky's hair as she stood by the car, glancing up and down the deserted street. All was quiet, apart from the gulls and the distant tinkling muzak of the funfair carousel.

"There's still power," said Larkin. "The lights are on, the funfair sounds operational... but there's no one here."

"It's like those abandoned places you see on the internet. You know, where there was a nuclear spill and everyone had to urgently leave their homes, and all the TVs are still on."

"You think that's what happened here?"

"No. And if so, it's the least of our worries. Come on, let's try one of the shops."

They crossed the road without checking for traffic, Becky leading the way, and entered THE RUMPLEJACK FRY, which, according to the sign, promised chips, fish suppers, and hot filled rolls. The interior was charmingly retro, with a bright blue counter and yellowing, tobacco-stained walls. There was an ashtray on the counter top, within which a lit cigarette smouldered.

Larkin eyed it suspiciously. "Is anybody here?"

No response was forthcoming.

"Check out those prices," said Becky, as she scanned the sign. "One-pound-forty for a fish supper. It's twelve pounds in my local."

"Thirty pence for a bag of chips?" said Larkin. "Fuck me, chips haven't been that price since—"

"1984, I'd be willing to bet."

They shared a knowing look, then left, walking next door to the gift shop. Inside, the trinkets and souvenirs — wooden replicas of the lighthouse, seashells with googly eyes on them — were priced similarly to the chippy, bringing Becky back to a time when she could buy a copy of

Bunty and a Freddo bar and still have change from her one pound pocket money.

A beaded curtain separated a staff room from the shop. Becky brushed through, finding a table with a cup of coffee on it, two seats, and a refrigerator. The fridge door was open, and inside—

"Larkin, get in here," she called.

"You can call me Gregor," he said, as he followed her into the staff room. "You don't need to—"

Then he saw it too.

The corpse in the fridge.

It was a man, his body bloated and naked, his knees tucked up to his chin. His head lolled back, exposing the ragged wound where his throat had been hacked away.

Larkin closed the fridge door and leaned against it. The colour had drained from his face. He looked at Becky. "You okay?"

"I'm not sure. That's not even the first corpse I've seen this month." She massaged her throat, wishing for a drink of water. "Do you ever get used to it?"

"No," he whispered, and offered her a troubled glance. "Hey, it's not too late to turn back."

"No, fuck that. I'm not leaving until I find my mum."

"And what about *him?*" asked Larkin, conspicuously avoiding using Tommy's name. "He lives here. What if he finds us?"

"Isn't that why you came? To find Tommy? To stop him?"

"Yeah," he said, sounding much less sure of himself than before. He reached into his jacket and pulled out a pistol, the black metal sparkling under the shop lights. "I guess it is."

25

Becky had never seen a gun in real life.

It was smaller than she expected, and more compact than the ones brandished by the likes of Jason Statham and Keanu Reeves in Hollywood blockbusters. She wondered if it would be enough to stop Tommy... if he even could be stopped.

She left the stifling atmosphere of the shop and took several breaths of fresh coastal air as she eyed the lighthouse. The imposing structure towered over Rumplejack the way Barad-dûr loomed over Mordor in her beloved *Lord of the Rings*.

"That's where we need to go," she said.

Larkin seemed unconvinced. He scratched at his temple with the barrel of the pistol, then noticed what he was doing and tucked the gun safely away. "We should find the police station first. There might be someone there, and I wouldn't mind some backup."

Becky nodded. There would be no one there, and Larkin likely already knew that, but if it would settle his nerves, there was no harm in trying. He sounded tense, and that concerned her. She needed his courage. She couldn't do this on her own.

"Okay," she said, and they walked along the street, glancing into the various empty shops they passed. The road forked, and they took the branch that led up the steep hill, climbing steadily upwards to where a crooked street sign pointed in two directions. In one, it promised a library, a nightclub, and public toilets. In the other?

"Police station," said Larkin, and he smiled for the first time since they had arrived in Rumplejack. They followed the sign until they found the station, a single-storey brick building nestled in the centre of a residential street. As they neared, Becky caught fleeting glimpses of movement in the surrounding buildings, but each time she turned to catch them, the faces vanished, and she saw only frayed lace curtains falling back into place.

They paused outside the station, peering through glass doors that had been wedged open with a lump of gnarled driftwood.

"There's someone in there," said Becky, squinting against the sunlight reflecting off the glass.

Larkin pulled the pistol from his jacket and gripped it in a tight fist. He moved closer, thumbing the safety off. "I see them."

He took the lead and entered first.

"Careful," said Becky.

He crept through the open door. "My name is Detective Constable Larkin, and I... *oh, fuck this.*"

"What?" Becky scurried in after him, expecting to find another bloated, mutilated corpse. When she saw what he was staring at, she almost laughed.

"Stick'emup," she whispered, moving nearer to the desk, behind which sat the tacky horse costume worn in the show by Rumplejack's resident cowboy. It looked even tattier than in the video, the fur moth-eaten, the stetson caked in dirt. Stick'emup's black eyes bored into her soul, and though she stepped to the side, the lifeless gaze seemed to follow her.

The rest of the room was empty save for three chairs lined up against the window, the desk, a bulky storage locker, and an attractive oil painting of Rumplejack lighthouse that hung above a metal door.

"There's no one here," she said. "There's no one *anywhere*. The whole town is—"

"Hello?"

A familiar, though unexpected, voice called to them.

Larkin held the gun away from his body, pointing it at the metal door. "It came from through there."

"Hello? Is someone there?"

Becky recognised the speaker, and she figured Larkin did too. From what he had told her, he had watched Rumplejack too many times to *not* recognise the voice of The Sausage King.

"It's that fucking bulldog puppet," said Larkin.

"Pug," said Becky. Larkin turned to her. She didn't like the way the gun trembled in his hand. "Not a bulldog."

She crossed the reception towards the door.

"You can't go in there." A new voice. Deeper, like a Scotsman doing a piss-poor John Wayne impersonation. *"Only the sheriff is allowed in there."*

She recognised that voice, too, and glanced at the cowboy costume sitting on the chair. From this angle, the desk no longer blocked her view, and she saw the axe lying on the floor by the cowboy's chunky plastic boots.

"Oh god," she said, as the costume rose from the chair and stooped to pick up the axe.

"Did you not hear me, pilgrim?" growled Stick'emup. "I'm the *sheriff* 'round these here parts!"

She turned to Larkin, who stood frozen as the cowboy lumbered forwards on his gangly legs, dragging the axe behind him.

"You new in town, stranger?"

"Please," said Becky, unsure of what to say. Could she reason with him? With a maniac dressed in a horse costume? "We're looking for—"

Stick'emup swung the axe at her, and she threw herself backwards as the blade split the air with a *whoosh*. She hit the ground and scrambled away, looking to Larkin for help.

"Stop right there," the detective murmured, taking a faltering step closer. "I'm... I'm a police officer."

Stick'emup turned to face him.

"Kill him!" shouted The Sausage King from through the door. *"Kill him while you have the chance!"*

But Larkin stood rigid with disbelief.

"Shoot him!" screamed Becky.

"A splendid suggestion!" yelled The Sausage King.

"Shut up!" Larkin shouted. "Everyone just shut up!"

Stick'emup raised his axe, poised to strike, and Larkin pulled the trigger.

Blood erupted from the back of the cowboy's suede waistcoat, spurting across the floor.

"Again!" screamed Becky, her ears ringing from the gunshot.

Stick'emup advanced on Larkin, seemingly unphased. The detective fired again, and again, each shot bursting from the horse costume in a fountain of blood that poured down his weathered jeans.

Nothing stopped him.

Stick'emup's axe whistled through the air, the blade

thudding into Larkin's arm. Bone broke, the snap as loud as the gunshots, and Larkin's weapon clattered to the ground. The cowboy dropped the axe and grabbed the detective by his collar, throwing him. He hit the desk and bounced over it, landing heavily on the other side.

The cowboy followed. "Tryin' to break into my jailhouse without so much as a howdy? You're gonna spend the rest of your life rotting in a cell, partner." He picked Larkin up again, this time shoving him into the locker. His head cracked off the metal, and when he collapsed forwards, the doors groaned open, revealing the contents.

Becky's eyes widened.

"Did you kill him? Is he dead yet?"

"Shut up, Sausage King!" she shouted, as she darted for the locker, slipping on the blood that gushed from Stick-'emup's torso. The cowboy was slowing. Each time he tossed Larkin across the room like a ragdoll, it took effort.

Becky seized her chance.

She gazed into the locker, at the axes and maces and clubs and daggers and swords and machetes and saws and hammers, and selected her weapon. A gleaming samurai sword. She imagined Jason Statham wielding it in the dreadful *In The Name Of The King,* and ran for the cowboy, surprised at how clear her mind was.

She brought the sword shrieking down, burying it next to the cowboy's spine. The wicked blade sliced through the costume, cleaving it apart and lodging in the flesh beneath.

"Well, shucks!" Stick'emup roared, turning to face her. He kicked out, connecting with her midsection and launching her against the wall. When Becky opened her eyes, she was on the floor and unable to breathe. She wanted to vomit, but her insides refused to comply. Stick-

'emup staggered towards her, rainbows of thick blood spraying from his bullet-riddled torso.

Then he stopped and tilted his head, staring at her through shiny, black eyes. "Jesus Christ," he said, dropping the John Wayne act and reverting to a broad Scots dialect. "It's you. It's really *you*."

"What?" she wheezed, trying and failing to stand.

"All this time, he's been searching... and now you waltz right in to Rumplejack on a silver platter." He shook his big horse head, the fabric ears flapping. "You stupid fucking cunt. You've doomed—"

A flash of light, and then Stick'emup's mouth widened in a silent scream. His head tilted back, exposing his jugular, where a thin red line had formed. Trickles of blood ran from the cut, and the wound opened further, arterial spray gushing down his waistcoat as the horse's head dropped from his shoulders and hit the floor, bouncing twice before coming to rest in the middle of the reception area. The body collapsed, revealing Larkin standing behind him, the samurai sword gripped in his sweaty, trembling hands. He released the weapon, letting it clatter to his feet, and stared at Becky.

"Is everything alright in there?" The Sausage King called. *"It's gone awfully quiet."*

Neither of them answered.

Becky managed to sit. Her ribs ached from the kick, but her breathing was improving. Unable to stand in the rapidly expanding puddle of gore, she crawled towards the downed cowboy's severed head, the jaws locked open in surprise.

"He recognised me," she said, blood soaking through her trousers, staining her hands. She looked at Larkin, who stared into space. "Get the gun," she said, and he dutifully retrieved it while she continued crawling towards the horse.

"What are you doing?" he asked.

"I need to know who it is."

"You know fine well who it is," the detective mumbled. "You've seen the fucking show."

"But who's wearing the costume?"

Larkin laughed at that, a laugh tinged with madness. "Aye, go on, take the mask off." He chuckled, and a tear rolled down his cheek. "See who's *wearing the costume.*"

She neared the head. The cowboy hat lay next to it, and she noticed it was made of cheap foam. She reached for the horse mask, amazed at the level of detail up close. The open jaw revealed yellowing teeth and a pink, dry tongue that...

"Go on," said Larkin. *"Take off the mask."*

But she couldn't. It was stuck. She nudged the head, and it slowly spun in the blood, giving her a perfect view of the neck.

"It's not a costume, is it Becky?" said Larkin. She couldn't tell if he was laughing or sobbing.

Blood oozed from the stump. The sword had severed it cleanly. So cleanly, in fact, that it was easy to see where the layer of fur and skin ended, and the muscle and bone began.

"You hear me?" Larkin leaned against the wall and slid into a crouch, covering his face with his hand. "It's not a fucking costume. It's *real.*"

26

"Jesus Christ," Larkin muttered, the words muffled by his hand. "Jesus fucking Christ."

Concerned, Becky watched him. The detective rubbed his eyes like a man emerging from a tomb and seeing daylight for the first time in years, while his broken arm hung by his side at a crooked angle, his jacket soaked in dark blood.

"Hey," she said, crawling towards him through the pool of spilled plasma. "It's okay, Gregor. He's dead now."

He laughed a low, sad chuckle and dipped his head, as if ashamed to be seen. "I thought I could handle it. I thought I could handle it, and I don't know if I can. It's, it's... y'know, Tommy is one thing." He took a breath, trying to compose himself. "He's a big man. A giant, even. But he's not—"

"A talking horse?"

He parted his fingers and looked at her through the splayed digits. "Exactly."

"Umm, hello? Is anybody there?"

"Oh god, the puppet," moaned Larkin. He laughed

again, and the hollow sound chilled her. "I forgot about the fucking *puppet.*"

"It's okay, I think he's on our side," she said, which did not appear to reassure him. She slid her way to the door and tried the handle. "We're okay," she called to The Sausage King. "But the door's locked."

"Stick'emup will have the key. I presume you've... disposed of him?"

"Christ," mumbled Larkin. "She's talking to it. She's talking to a puppet."

Becky ignored him and glanced at the severed horse head. "Yeah. We killed him. We fucked him right up." She looked at Larkin. "Didn't we?"

"Guess so," he said, offering a half-hearted shrug.

"Fetch the key, please!"

Carefully, Becky made her way back to the cowboy. The keys were hooked onto Stick'emup's belt, and she wrestled them free and returned to the door, pausing in front of Larkin. "Are you coming? Or are you going to sit on your arse a bit longer?"

She didn't mean to be so blunt, but this was not the time to fuck around.

"Yeah, yeah," he mumbled. "Help me up."

She offered a hand, trying not to look at the way his blood-soaked arm turned back on itself.

"I need to go to hospital," he said.

She inserted the key and unlocked the door. "I know. Soon."

"No, Becky." He held his arm up and let it dangle. *"Now."*

"You think Tommy won't find you there?"

Larkin started to protest, and she cut him off.

"He almost killed you before, and that was in the middle

of a police station. He'll find you wherever you go, don't you understand that? We're close. We're *so* close."

"To what?"

"I don't know! Finding out how we can stop him?" She turned her back on him and opened the door. "Or finding out what he wants."

Stale air seeped from inside the room, the stench of atrocities and decay slathering itself over her skin. She covered her nose and mouth and crossed the threshold, leaving Larkin lurking in the doorway.

"Hello there," said The Sausage King. "I'm very glad to see you. Do you have any sausages?"

Becky took one look at the puppet, and said to Larkin, "Maybe wait outside for a minute."

There were two corpses in the cell. One was an enormous cuddly teddy that she recognised from the show as Silly Bear. He lay on his back, his chest torn open, cracked bones jutting out. Becky recoiled at the sight of thousands of maggots squirming inside the cavity.

There's your smell.

The second corpse was a human male. He was naked, and missing both legs and an arm, which lay festering on the floor. His skin was dark and rotten, but his remaining arm was raised to the ceiling, and on the end perched the pug hand puppet known as The Sausage King.

"Well?" he asked. "Do you have any sausages? I'm awfully hungry."

"No," she said. "No sausages."

"That is a shame. It's been so long since I've had any sausages. A Sausage King without any sausages is a melancholy king indeed."

"I'm losing my fucking mind," said Larkin from the doorway.

Becky glared at him. "I told you to wait outside."

"Oh!" said The Sausage King. "Another friend! Do *you* have sausages?"

With a lop-sided grin, Larkin made an elaborate show of checking his pockets. "Guess I'm all out, little buddy."

"Sarcasm," said The Sausage King. "How very droll." His round head pivoted towards Becky on the dead man's wrist. "Would you mind trying the keys in my cell door? It gets terribly lonely in here. Especially at night, when I can hear the screams echoing across the bay."

She tried each key, one after another, to no avail.

"Oh, bother," said The Sausage King. "Thank you for trying, anyway. I suppose *he* has them."

"You mean Tommy?"

"Of course."

Larkin staggered to the bars, his dazed expression turning to one of anger. "What do you know about him? He's after me. He wants to kill me."

"I'm not surprised. I've just met you, and I *also* want you dead."

"Fuck you, Muppet."

"Stop arguing, both of you," said Becky. She turned back to the puppet, consciously avoiding focusing on the carnage that surrounded him. "Does Tommy live in the lighthouse?"

"Why, of course! Are you planning on paying him a visit?"

"Yeah."

"My, how pleasant. You will say hello to your mother for me, won't you?"

The words stunned her. She had to play them again in her mind, processing them. "My... mother?"

"Indeed. She lives in the lighthouse with Tommy. She's his best friend." The puppet paused. "He's not *her* best friend, though. In fact, I'm not sure she likes him much at all. But time passes, and, much like the seasons, people change."

The room swam. Becky gripped the bars to remain upright. "She's still alive?"

"I couldn't say, I'm afraid. Tommy locked me up a long time ago. He's rotten."

"Wait, wait... how did you..." — she blinked, and wanted more than anything to cry — "...how do you know who I am?"

"You've been here before. Don't you remember?" The puppet sighed. "I suppose, you *were* just a child then. You were very kind to me. You brought me sausages, and then I ate the sausages. A grand time was had by all."

"This is ridiculous," said Larkin. "Everyone is fucking insane."

"Stop it, please!" said Becky. She looked The Sausage King in his strange, sad eyes. "I'm going to the lighthouse. If I find the key, I'll come back and let you out. I promise."

"That *would* be nice. Good luck, Rebecca. You'll need it." He seemed to smile at her. "And that's the woof."

"Goodbye, Sausage King."

She waved, and followed Larkin out of the door. As they left, she heard The Sausage King calling after her.

"If you don't find the key, I'd appreciate some sausages. I miss sausages."

"I'll do my best," she said, and left the station in a daze. Outside, the sunlight stung her eyes, and she shielded them, gazing along the coast to the lighthouse as she and Larkin walked back down to the main street, unsure of what to say to each other. Blood dripped from the detective's arm, dotting the pavement. His face was pale.

"Are you okay to drive?" she asked. Larkin kept walking, his jaw clenched. "Gregor? I asked if you're okay to drive?"

He stopped, and turned to her. "I heard you the first time."

She didn't understand his tone. Was he angry? "Then why didn't you answer?"

"Because we've got a problem."

She took an exasperated breath. "What now? What the *fuck* could possibly make this worse?"

He smiled unpleasantly at her, and looked further down the road. "How about that?"

Becky followed his gaze. "Oh, shit."

"Yup," he said, gazing into the distance towards their car. "Looks like we've got company."

27

Dressed in denim dungarees and a floral shirt, and with her hair in a loose perm, the woman wandered around Larkin's vehicle, occasionally stopping to check her surroundings and furtively test the doorhandles. Upon finding them locked, she would circle the car and try again, performing the same actions repeatedly, as if somehow expecting a different outcome on her seventh or eighth attempt.

"I don't like this," said Larkin.

"It's just one woman."

"One that we can *see.*"

"You have a gun, Gregor."

"It's out of ammo."

"Didn't you bring any spare?"

"Of course I did." He bit his lip. "It's in the glove compartment."

"Shit." She looked up at the surrounding buildings, where pale, haunted faces watched from the windows. "Hey—"

"I see them. Act naturally, like we've not noticed."

Acting naturally did not come easily to Becky, but she tried, painfully aware of every step she took, of each swing of her arms. "Once we're in the car," she said, "we can be at the lighthouse in a couple of minutes."

"Or we could get the hell out of town, go back to Edinburgh, and come back here with fifty armed officers."

"They'd never believe us."

"Then we'll make something up. We'll tell them—"

"I'm not leaving, Gregor. Did you not hear him? The Sausage King said—"

"Do you hear *yourself?*" he snarled. *"The Sausage King said?* Jesus, you're as crazy as they are."

The words hurt her. People had called her crazy before, but usually not people she liked, and certainly not people she had slept with.

He's scared, and lashing out.

Sure, but he didn't have to take it out on her.

"I don't care about Tommy," he continued. "So what if we find him? What are going to do, drive a stake through his heart? This whole town is fucked. We just killed a talking horse, and now you're taking directions from a puppet." He turned away from her. "I'm sorry, Becky. I'm getting out of here, and I hope you come with me. Because if not, I'll—"

Glass smashed.

They looked to the car, where the woman had punched her fist through the window.

"Oh, fuck this," said Larkin, and he took off towards his car. "Hey! What the hell are you doing?"

The woman looked at him like a child caught stealing. Blood oozed from several deep slices in her hand. "I'm sorry," she said. "I didn't know who it belonged to."

"So you thought you'd break the window?"

She didn't answer. Instead, she trailed her fingers along

the bonnet, caressing the smooth metal. "It's been so long since I've seen one."

"Keep your hands off," said Larkin.

She looked at him, her blood running down the paintwork. "Take me with you. Please. They won't let me leave. I don't belong here. It's *them*. They're the ones who're crazy, not me."

"Oi, you lot," said a new voice.

Becky and Larkin turned to see a burly man in white overalls striding towards them. He smiled, but the smile was unnatural, as if he had forgotten how. "Where you cunts headed? Up the coast? It's been a wee while since I was up there. Fancy taking me for a drive? I won't be any bother."

"They're taking *me*," hissed the woman. "So fuck off, Jacob."

"Sorry," said Larkin. "We're going straight to the hospital. As you can see," he said, holding his arm up, "I had a run-in with a talking horse earlier. I cut his fucking head off."

"Gregor," whispered Becky, but he wasn't finished.

"Now, I suggest you both fuck right off to the other side of the street before the same happens to you."

More were coming. Becky noticed them first, Rumplejack's dishevelled and forgotten residents appearing in doorways, their dead eyes blinking in the sunshine.

"I think we need to leave," she said to Larkin.

"Great idea!" said the woman, and she tried to climb through the broken window, getting halfway through before Larkin hauled her out by her dungarees. There was a ghastly tearing sound as her belly scratched across the shards of glass embedded in the frame, and when he shoved her out of the way, blood flowed from deep gashes in her stomach.

"Okay," the burly resident in the overalls said. "Let's go before the others—"

Larkin punched the man. He hit the ground, his head cracking against the tarmac.

"Get in the fucking car," Larkin barked, hitting the burton on his keys to unlock the vehicle. At the shrill sound of the beeps, a collective roar erupted from all around.

The people of Rumplejack had spoken.

Some carried weapons, others ran with their heads down, but all headed towards a single destination.

The car.

"Oh, fuck," said Becky. She raced to the passenger door and leaped in, brushing as much of the shattered glass from the seat as possible. Larkin threw the door open and entered, not caring about the glass. He rummaged for his keys and tried the engine.

It wouldn't start.

"Fucking flood water," he grumbled, and tried again.

Becky watched through the window.

The residents were closing in.

"Hurry!" she shouted.

"I'm fucking trying!"

The engine roared into life as a plank of wood, wielded by a resident, smacked against the door with a fearsome thud. Larkin slammed the accelerator down and the car lurched forwards, the mob giving chase, hurling stones and makeshift missiles. A can of beans smashed through the back windscreen, but a glance in the rearview mirror confirmed that the townspeople had no hope of catching them.

"Fucking crazies," said Larkin with a lunatic gleam in his eye. "Bunch of fucking *crazies.*"

The car sped along the narrow road, leaving Rumplejack

and its mysteries behind as the lighthouse loomed closer on the horizon. They would pass it soon. They would pass it, and it would be gone forever.

"We need to stop at the lighthouse," said Becky.

Larkin kept his eyes locked on the winding track. "Are you kidding me? We barely got out of there alive."

"We *have* to. My mum's in there."

"You don't know that."

They skidded around a corner, the lighthouse drawing closer.

"That's why we have to check! What if she's in there? What if she needs help?"

"I'm not stopping."

"Gregor, you have to! You fucking have to!" Her vision clouded, a migraine building. "Stop the car and let me out! You don't even have to come in, you can wait in the car." She punched her leg to punctuate her words. *"But let me the fuck out!"*

"Fine!" he yelled, swerving onto a dirt track that led to the tall building. "Get yourself killed!" The car screeched to a stop, and he stared at her. "I'll wait for you, okay? But at the first sign of trouble, I'm out of here, understand? I'm gone. I won't wait, Becky. If it comes down to it... I'll leave you here. I'll fucking leave you."

Becky stared back at him, forcing herself to make eye contact. "Yeah, sooner or later, everybody does." She opened the door and stormed out, jogging down the remaining track towards the lighthouse. It was huge, and standing so close made it feel like a skyscraper. The sea crashed all around, and as she looked up to the lamp, night fell. It happened in an instant, the sky darkening, the sun collapsing into the horizon like a deflated balloon. An icy wind blasted her, and she shivered before the wooden door.

The car idled behind her. She wished Larkin would come inside, even if only for the protection of his gun. Should she ask to borrow it? Would he let her?

Fuck it. There was no time.

And if you knock on the big wooden door…

Becky rubbed her eyes, took one last look around, and pushed the door.

It was unlocked.

"Tommy will gut you like a whore," she breathed, and went inside.

28

Larkin watched her enter the lighthouse with a sinking sensation in his gut.

They should be getting the fuck outta town, not stopping to investigate. He knew she was on a mission to locate her mother, and that it was important to her... but staying alive was *also* very important. Some would say *essential*.

He scratched at his chin and remembered he hadn't shaved in two days. Christ, did that matter? No, but it was a normal thing for a normal person to think, and right now, Larkin longed for normality. He paced around the car, watching the town, seeking movement. Nothing so far. But they would come. He knew they would.

Shit, this couldn't be real. It couldn't, it wouldn't, it *shouldn't* be real.

The puppet had been the last straw. The fucking Sausage King. It was too much. He could accept Tommy, because the unstoppable giant lay within the realm of possibility. He was unusual. Unlikely, even. But *possible*.

As for the cowboy... a real-life talking horse, who walked on his hind legs and ran a police station? Who kept an armoury of torture devices in a locker? *That* had almost sent Larkin over the edge. At first, the incomprehensible terror had shaken him, and only the life-or-death struggle to survive, to *kill,* brought him back from the brink. After fifteen years on the force, he understood survival. It steadied him, centred him, gave him a sense of purpose and balance.

The puppet, though? On the arm of a dead man? Demanding sausages?

That was too much.

It was too bizarre, too insane. Too... silly?

Yes, it was *silly*. And while Larkin processed violence and brutality and devastation and grief every day at work, he couldn't wrap his mind around a plane of existence where an inanimate puppet handed out quests like a video game NPC.

It just didn't... fucking... happen.

He wanted out of here. To return to Edinburgh and contact the military and get this infernal place wiped off the map for good. He had killed the cowboy, and that proved something. These motherfuckers could *die*. With the right amount of ammunition, and a whole lot of help, he could take down Tommy. But not alone. Unlike Becky, he didn't dare face him alone.

"You're a brave woman," he said, looking up at the towering white building, before glancing back at the town. From far away, myriad light sources flickered in the darkness.

Fire.

"Oh, fuck me," he said, squinting through the night as the people of Rumplejack amassed on the main street, flaming torches held aloft like angry villagers seeking Frankenstein's monster. They set off, taking the road out of town that led to the lighthouse. Larkin gauged the distance and figured they would arrive in ten minutes, tops.

He gripped his gun, holding it to his chest, and wondered how much longer Becky would be.

"You'd better hurry your arse up," he said, watching as the fiery mass approached. "Or I'm fucking out of here."

∽

The lighthouse was quiet.

The wooden door had led into a passageway, from which stone steps spiralled up. Becky tip-toed up them, trying to ignore the rancid odour of spoiled meat that seeped from above. She entered an empty storeroom with a narrow ladder in the centre. The stench here was overpowering, and, fighting against every instinct, she walked to the ladder. Dark red stains coated the wooden steps, and she climbed to the next level, preparing herself for—

She gagged.

Bodies. So many bodies. They were piled against the curved walls, stacked atop each other in various stages of decomposition. Some were skeletons, others had withered like dead flowers. The bodies on top were fresher, and their rank odour caused Becky to finally — after all she had seen — vomit. She tried to retch quietly, but that proved impossible.

Only two floors remained before the lamp room. She thought back to the opening credits. What came next? A living space, then a bedroom. Her mum had to be in one of those rooms. And, by that logic, so did Tommy. The next ladder was over by the wall, the floors separated by a closed wooden hatch. Wiping spittle from her lips, Becky started to climb, eager to be free of the fetid stench. She hoped the hatch would be unlocked.

It was.

The faint buzz of static filled the next room, the blue light from an old-fashioned television dancing across the round walls. She emerged from the hatch, transfixed by the glow of the telly. The sound was muted, but an episode of Rumplejack was playing, the imagery drawing her onwards as if in a trance.

It was the opening credits, but they were different. *Two figures approached the lighthouse, and neither were the usual woman.* She recognised one of them immediately.

Tommy.

His hulking shape dominated the frame, and he stooped low to hold hands with the second figure, a little girl in a yellow dress and white sandals. The girl skipped merrily alongside Tommy, and before it cut to a close-up of her smiling face, Becky knew she was looking at herself. That dress had been her favourite. It was still in the attic, marred by bloodstains that her father had insisted were from when she had fallen out of a tree.

"But dad, I don't remember falling out of a tree," she had said to him once, to which he had nodded sagely, and said, *"Exactly."*

Then her young face filled the frame, and Becky knelt before the TV as if in prayer. She touched the screen and felt a faint jolt of electricity crackle through her fingertips.

"So you found me," said a woman's voice.

Becky's heart almost stopped. Her head swooned, and she wasn't sure she had the strength to turn around. But turn she did, and there, in a red leather chair that had seen better days, sat Meredith Tremayne.

Her mother.

Sitting cross-legged, the woman looked her daughter up and down.

"You couldn't stay away, could you?" she said with a gentle shake of her head. "Oh Rebecca... why couldn't you *just stay away?*"

29

Rumplejack's residents were drawing nearer.

Larkin waited by the car, watching in mounting panic as they approached. The engine was running, and he had reloaded his pistol with the remaining bullets, which, by his calculations, meant he had one bullet for every three maniacs. There were good odds, there were bad odds, and then there were *you're fucked* odds.

The men and women marched onwards, never pausing, their torches sparking in front of grim, ashen faces. They would be here soon. In a matter of minutes, going by their current trajectory. Larkin leaned into the car and hovered his hand over the horn. He looked up at the lighthouse.

"Come on, Becky, where the fuck are you?"

Time was almost up.

∽

"Mum?"

"Hush, Rebecca," her mother hissed. "He's upstairs. Do you want to wake him?"

"I don't understand," was all she could say. Words, as they so often did, had temporarily abandoned her.

Her mother's stern face softened, and a tear rolled down her gaunt cheek. "I'm sorry," she said. "I prayed this day would never come, that you'd never find the tapes. You *did* find them, didn't you?"

Becky closed her eyes in concentration, forcing the words out. "They were in the wall. If you didn't want me to find them, why did you keep them in the house?"

"They found their way back. No matter what we did with them, or where we put them, they *always* found their way back. What we decided — your father and I — was to hide them close to you. It was the only thing that seemed to work." She looked at Becky with plaintive eyes. "How is he?"

There was too much information, too much going on. She struggled to follow.

"Who?"

"Your father. Is he..."

"He's dead. We buried him yesterday."

Christ, was it only the day before? It felt like a lifetime ago.

Becky's mother nodded to herself, as if expecting as much.

"Mum, I've missed you so badly. Where have you been?"

"I've been here. With Tommy."

Becky rubbed her face, rubbed it raw. "What... but... *why?*"

"It was *you* he wanted. I stole you back from him and took your place. He wasn't happy about it. He's still not happy."

"But who *is* he?" A headache throbbed all the way from her eyeballs to the base of her neck. "And why does he want me?"

"Keep your voice down. If he hears—"

The car horn blared from outside. Two short blasts, followed by a third, which went on for a good ten seconds. It ended abruptly, and Becky ran to the nearest window. She gazed down at the car, at Larkin frantically signalling, and at the mob of torch-wielding citizens closing in on the lighthouse.

She turned to her mother. "They're coming for us."

The woman smiled. "Ah, the citizens of Rumplejack. Some think they can escape and return to their old lives. Others believe that when the Prodigal Daughter returns, he'll let the rest of us die. But I think they're all wrong."

A dull thud echoed from the floor above.

"He won't let us leave. Any of us."

Another thud, heavy footsteps pounding throughout the lighthouse.

Her mother wiped the tears from her eyes. "You have to go now, Rebecca," she said, and looked up at the ceiling. "Tommy's awake."

30

"No, no, I can't go. I *won't go*," cried Becky. "I just *found* you!"

"And it's been lovely," said her mum. "It's been wonderful. A dream." She stood and held Becky's face in her hands. "You've grown from a beautiful, strong-willed little girl into a beautiful, strong-willed woman. I knew you would." She smiled sadly. "And I'm glad you had the chance."

The footsteps clomped along the ceiling.

Outside, someone fired a gun.

Becky flinched at the harsh report. "Mum, please, come with us. I can't lose you again, I've got so much to tell you, so much to—"

"It's you or me, Becky. That was the deal. And I wanted you to live your life. I love you, Becky." She kissed her daughter, and Becky gripped her in a hug, her adrenaline spiking as she hovered on the verge of a meltdown. "I'm just happy I got to see you… one last time."

The trapdoor in the ceiling burst open.

The smile fell from her mum's face. "Go," she said. *"Now."*

Wracked by indecision, Becky hesitated.

Her mother shoved her. "I said go! I'll try to hold him off!"

A huge foot appeared through the hatch.

Tommy will gut you like a whore.

"Go!" her mother screamed, and Becky turned and ran. She reached the ladder and climbed down, her foot slipping and sending her crashing to the floor beneath. She heard commotion upstairs.

"It's not her, Tommy! I swear, it's not her. Please, leave her alone! For god's sake..."

Then Becky heard her no more, the stone walls of the oil room blotting out any stray sounds. She passed the corpses and took the ladder to the storeroom. Why couldn't she breathe? Why the fuck couldn't she breathe?

You're hyperventilating.

Yes, that was it. And there was fuck all she could do about it as she careened down the spiral staircase. Would Larkin be waiting for her? *I'm coming,* she wanted to shout, but her lungs were at full capacity. Her shoulder scraped against the rough brick wall as she hurriedly descended, until at last the final passageway was visible.

Come on, come on!

She took the last step and hurtled around the corner, racing through the open doorway. The frigid night air hit her like a slap.

"Get in!" screamed Larkin. He had turned the car, and stood by it, the doors open and waiting. The townsfolk were closing in fast, and he rested his one good arm on the open door and fired into the crowd.

Glass shattered high above, and Becky looked up in time to see a body sail through the air. It came crashing down headfirst on the track and slumped into a miserable heap of broken bones.

"No!"

She ran to the crumpled body — her *mother's* body — and knelt. The impact had flattened the woman's cranium, and blood poured from her mouth and nose. She was barely recognisable.

"Becky, get the fuck in the fucking car right fucking now!" roared Larkin.

But she couldn't move. A lifetime of feeling lost and abandoned, of wondering where her mother was... and suddenly, after the briefest of reunions, it was over. All over. Her mother was gone. Dead.

Dead, dead, dead.

A hand on her shoulder.

She screamed and looked up into the face of Gregor Larkin.

"Get up!" he yelled, hauling her to her feet. She stood on useless legs that failed to support her weight, and looked at the car. The townspeople had almost reached it.

I can't, she tried to say, the words catching in her throat. *He killed her.*

Larkin tucked the gun into his waistband and hooked his arm around her, dragging her towards the car. Someone threw their torch, and it whistled past his face as he bundled Becky into the passenger seat. He drew his gun, firing the remaining bullets at the advancing citizens as he made his way around the vehicle and clambered in.

"You ready?" he shouted.

She could only nod.

He killed her. Tommy killed her.

She shifted her body, looking back through the rear

windshield as Tommy emerged from the lighthouse like a ravenous ghoul.

You bastard, she wanted to shout, if only her brain would let her. *You killed my mum!*

Larkin hit the gas, and the car shot towards the townspeople. "You'd better fucking move," he grunted, and most did, flinging themselves to the side to avoid the oncoming vehicle. The remaining foolhardy souls hit the bumper. Bones snapped and popped as the car ploughed into them, bodies smacking against the windscreen and sliding over the roof, hitting the dirt as the car picked up speed.

Becky looked in the wing mirror, watching as Tommy stepped over her mother's body and lumbered after them.

"We did it!" shouted Larkin. "We fucking *did it!*"

He spun the wheel, taking a sharp turn, his laughter mixing with tears. Becky wondered if, after all this, he'd ever be the same again.

"Did you find her?" he asked.

"Huh?"

"Your mum! You find her?"

"No," she said quietly. She picked up Grumpus and hugged the cuddly toy, pressing his fur to her cheek. She couldn't talk about her mother. She wanted to, but she couldn't. Not now. Maybe not ever.

"I'm sorry," said Larkin. "I really am sorry to hear that." He broke out in a grin. "But hey, we're still alive! Jesus, I almost left, you know. I said I would, and I nearly did. But I waited! I waited for you, and I used the horn, and—"

The windscreen exploded.

The pane of glass seemed to collapse in on itself, breaking into thousands of tiny shards that spilled into the car like a sparkling wave of vomit.

Becky looked at Larkin, at his shattered face with the wide hole punched in it, blood jetting violently across the dashboard, his hands spasming arrhythmically on the steering wheel. Thin wisps of smoke drifted from the back of his head, and when he slumped forwards, leaking bone and crimson gore onto his lap, she saw the sizzling hole in the vehicle seat headrest.

The car rolled to a stop, and only then did Becky manage to scream.

"You, in the car," boomed a loud voice. *"Turn around and go back the way you came."*

It took Becky a moment to realise the voice was coming through a loudspeaker. She looked ahead, through the crumbling remains of the windscreen, and saw the fence. Two military-style trucks were positioned alongside it, and on top of one lay a man, his sniper rifle trained on her.

RYLAK CORPORATION was printed on the side of one of the trucks.

"You have twenty seconds, or we will be forced to open fire."

Becky sat still, hugging her penguin and listening to the wet splatter of blood from Larkin's slack, dead body.

They had killed him.

Why? Why had they done this? What the fuck? Why did everyone around her have to die?

"You now have fifteen seconds to comply. Turn the car around and go back the way you came."

Becky sat trembling in her seat. Should she get out? How could she turn the car around if she didn't know how to drive?

The sniper fired again. The bullet struck the roof of the car with a deafening *clang,* and Becky scrambled down into the vehicle's footrest, clutching her penguin like a safety blanket.

"That was your final warning," said the man with the loudspeaker in his firm, clear voice. *"You now have ten seconds turn the vehicle around."*

But if she went back to the lighthouse, she would die!

A moan escaped her lips. She didn't know what to do. Curled up by Larkin's feet, her head inches from the pedals, Becky peed her pants. She hated herself as she did, and clenched her fists in righteous anger.

"Fuck... *you,*" she said.

They had done this to her. They had killed Gregor, and they would kill her too. From the strange men on the other side of the fence, to Tommy, to the townspeople... it seemed *everyone* wanted to hurt her — to kill her — and she was done with it.

She was fucking *sick* of it.

Sick of being mistreated, of being made a fool of, of being bullied and threatened and discriminated against by people who didn't understand her, who didn't *care* about her, who saw her as disposable and a nuisance and a pathetic waste of time. She was a person, too, dammit. A human being who could make her *own* fucking decisions.

She peered up over the dashboard and stared through the broken windscreen.

"You have five seconds to comply. This is your last chance."

"Damn right it is," she whispered.

She had no choices left to make, no more options. Death stalked her on all sides, and there was only one way out. One last desperate chance at survival.

She was going to have to Statham it.

And though she couldn't drive, and didn't fully understand how cars worked, she knew the engine was still running, and that—

"Fuck you!" she shouted, dropping back into the footrest and slamming both hands down on the pedal.

She heard the sniper open fire, metal striking metal as bullets punched through the car, the seats exploding in bursts of scorched polyester. Becky screamed and closed her eyes as the car shot forwards. How would she know when she was through the gate? She supposed—

Crash!

The fence offered no resistance, the car smashing through it and hitting one of the trucks, knocking Becky's vehicle off-course. She peered up from her low vantage point and saw a tangle of wire fence draped over the window.

Releasing the pedal, she pushed Larkin upright and perched herself on his bloodsoaked lap, his annihilated face dripping down her back like melted ice cream. She pressed her foot to the accelerator, spinning the wheel to get back on track. Bright lights flooded behind her.

The other truck was giving chase.

"Jesus fucking Christ," she said, her eyes unblinking, electricity surging through her limbs. *"Leave me alone!"*

Her headlights were dim. She knew there was a switch somewhere to brighten them, but not where to find it.

Keep your mind on the road!

The bends came at her quickly. How fast was she going? Should she slow down? She pressed the brake pedal too hard, the car slowing dramatically and throwing her against the steering wheel as the onrushing headlights of the truck illuminated the interior.

They were going to hit her.

At the last second, the truck driver swerved to avoid the collision. Wheels screeched and the vehicle tipped. It crashed onto its side and scraped along the tarmac at high speed, shooting up sparks before ripping through the roadside barrier and dropping out of sight.

"I'm sorry!" shouted Becky.

Then she hit the gas, throwing the car forwards, and sped on through the night, leaving the hellish memory of Rumplejack far, far behind.

31

It was daylight when she awoke, the sky a dull grey. Rain streamed in through the broken windscreen, drenching her. She heard talking, and groggily opened her eyes, her vision swimming in and out of focus. Several people in high-vis jackets loitered outside the car.

Police officers. For the first time in her life, Becky was happy to see them.

Had she crashed? She couldn't recall. Everything was a blur after the truck had overturned, though her aching body told her that, *yeah,* she had most likely crashed.

An officer stood nearby, talking into her radio. "We've located the vehicle. The suspects are inside."

Suspects? There had to be a mistake. What did they suspect her of? Wearily, Becky reached for the handle and opened the door.

"Don't move!"

A second officer arrived on the scene carrying an extendable baton. They seemed to be keeping their distance. Did they regard her as a threat? God, it was almost funny.

"Approach with caution," ordered a voice on the radio.

The first officer yanked the door fully open. "Good god," she said, as she hauled Becky out of the vehicle. Larkin's destroyed face was stuck to her back, and his corpse came tumbling out after her as the cop forced her onto the wet ground.

"Stop!" Becky cried. "What are you—"

"Shut up!"

"But I didn't—"

The officer struck her between her shoulder blades with the baton. Pain flared down her jolted spine.

"Rebecca Sharp, you are wanted in connection with, uh, *multiple* murders. You do not have to say anything, but it may harm your defence if you do not mention, when questioned, something which you later rely on in court."

"What murders? What are you talking about?" She screamed the words, thrashing her body to escape their firm grip.

The officer talked over her. "Anything you do say may be given in evidence."

"What fucking murders? I haven't killed anyone!"

The officers wrestled her hands behind her, snapping the handcuffs on tight enough to cut into her circulation.

"Jesus Christ," said the second cop. "Is that DC Larkin?"

"It used to be," replied the first officer, before she cracked Becky over the head with her baton and everything went dark.

PART III

32

The lights in the interrogation room stung her eyes.

"Please, I have to go to the bathroom," said Becky. She didn't need to pee; she needed some time out, a moment of respite from her interrogators. They had been at it for hours. The questions, the accusations, the demands, the threats. She sat at a table on an uncomfortable wooden chair, her handcuffs threaded through a metal bar affixed to the tabletop.

"Not yet, Mrs Sharp," said a bearded man who had identified himself as Officer Greco. "Not until you answer our questions." He spoke softly, the two men playing the old good cop, bad cop routine that Becky thought was an invention of the movies.

"My partner's right," said the other man — Fuller was his name — as he smacked his fist off the table, causing her cup of water to spill. "Tell us the truth, and this can all be over. It's up to you."

"I told you—"

"Okay, how about this?" interrupted Greco. "Let's say you *didn't* kill Andrew Malcolm in his place of business."

"Andy's Laser Emporium," said Fuller.

"And let's also say you didn't kill your father, which is the only plausible part of your story. He had a heart attack, maybe that was bad luck." He paused. "Or maybe that was what set you off? The guilt, the trauma... is that why you killed your husband and your sister? Or was it because you found out they were sleeping together?"

"We know you killed them," Fuller interjected. "We just want to know *why*. Why'd you do it, Becky? Revenge? A jealous rage?"

"I didn't kill them," she whispered. "I didn't even know they were dead until this morning."

"She seems real broken up about it," said Fuller dismissively, and then it was Greco's turn.

"It's a funny coincidence, isn't it? We find dozens of apologetic texts sent from your husband's phone to yours, and then he turns up dead. We even found a note from him that says — and I quote — *'like you, I sometimes lose control of my emotions.'* Like you, huh? You often lose control, Mrs Sharp?"

"That was different. He'd stolen my laptop, and—"

"You killed him over that?"

"I didn't kill him! I told you, it was—"

"Rotten Tommy. Yeah, you said that already."

"He's the giant, right?" asked Fuller. "The bald giant with the head made out of dough?"

"I didn't say it was *made* of dough," said Becky. "I said it looked like—"

"Now, he's not to be confused with The Sandwich King, am I right? The talking puppet?"

"The *Sausage* King," she corrected, instantly regretting it. She should never have mentioned Rumplejack. What the fuck had she been thinking? Except the problem was, she *hadn't* been thinking. She was doped up on painkillers, and should be resting in bed. They had no right to do this. Shouldn't she have a lawyer?

"So let me get this straight, Mrs Sharp," said Fuller. "You claim you and Detective Constable Larkin were off chasing ghosts together, because of a haunted video you found in your wall, and while you were away, a magic giant killed your sister and your husband."

"No, I—"

"And in a ghost town that isn't on any map, you killed a talking horse, met a sentient hand puppet, found your *dead mother* hiding in a lighthouse, and ran away from the aforementioned giant while my colleague Detective Constable Larkin was accidentally shot in the face during your getaway?"

"No, well... yes, some of that is true, but Gregor wasn't shot accidentally, he—"

"So you admit it? You killed him?"

"I didn't fucking kill him!" she shouted, rattling the chain of her handcuffs. "Why won't you let me finish?"

"Temper, temper," Greco admonished. The two men fell silent, letting the room breathe.

If they were trying to confuse her, they were doing a damn fine job. What she wished for, more than anything, was the velvety embrace of Grumpus. But her penguin friend was likely still in Larkin's car. He was — like everyone else in her life — gone for good.

"Listen," said Becky, her temples pounding. "You claim I killed John and Flora the night he sent those texts, right? Well, I was with Gregor—"

"Call him Detective Constable Larkin," said Fuller. "Show some respect to the man you killed."

She drew in a breath, and continued. "I was with Detective Constable Larkin that night."

"*All* night?"

She lowered her eyes to the table. "Yes. All night."

"Gee, it's a pity he's too *dead* to corroborate that convenient alibi. Do you have any other witnesses? Preferably ones you haven't murdered?"

She tried to think. She had waited in the car while Larkin booked the room. No one had seen her there. No one but…

"Yes! Yes, I have witnesses. Two men, at The Beechburn Institute. A doctor, whose name I don't know, and a patient called Horsham-Blake. *Quintin* Horsham-Blake."

Greco smiled at this information. "Oh, we know all about your little sojourn to the Beechburn Institute, Mrs Sharp. We've seen the photos of the aftermath. *A bloodbath,* one of my colleagues described it as. *The work of a psychopath,* said another."

Becky sat, stunned. When had this happened?

"Okay," she said, panic building. "So you're saying I killed my family and the people in the hospital on the same night? How's that possible?"

Good thinking. You got them there.

"The same night?" said Fuller, a frown creasing his brow. "We never said that. The killings were three days apart."

"Now *you're* not making sense," said Becky. She had them on the back foot now! *They* were the ones who were confused, and *they* had their dates wrong. "We only left Edinburgh a couple of days ago. So how could I be in two places at once?"

The policeman looked at her with deadpan faces.

"A couple of days ago?" Greco smirked. "Mrs Sharp, you've been wanted for the murder of your husband and sister for *ten days*. There's been a manhunt combing the length of the country for you. Your face has been in the papers and on the news for the last week." He leaned in close. "You're *famous*. But what I'd like to know is, where the hell were you hiding, and what were you doing with *my friend's dead body?*" He roared the last few words, his cheeks reddening with fury.

Ten days... it was impossible. They had been gone two nights. One was spent in the Bed and Breakfast, the other in the crashed car. But ten days? No, absolutely not. No way. No fucking way.

"Do you take drugs, Mrs Sharp?" asked Fuller, his voice calm as he seized the Good Cop mantle from Greco.

"No, never."

"Never? You've never even taken any medication?"

"I have in the past, for my anxiety, but not—"

"Oh, that's right, you're autistic, aren't you? Tell me, does that condition give you super strength?"

"Are you able to rip a man apart?" asked Greco.

"You ever get confused, Mrs Sharp?"

"You ever want to hurt someone?"

"You ever lose control?"

"You don't just kill people, do you, Mrs Sharp?"

"You want to hurt them."

"Do you hear voices?"

"Do they tell you to kill?"

"What about the giant? Does he speak to—"

"Stop!" she screamed, hammering her fists off the table, the cuffs digging into her wrists. *"Stop it! Stop, stop, stop!"* She was making a scene, but she couldn't help it. They were trying to stress her, make her say or do something incriminating... and it was working. God, she wanted Grumpus so badly right now.

"I understand why you killed your family," said Fuller. "But why the doctors? What did you do with their intestines?"

She couldn't answer. She couldn't even breathe. Sickness rose in her stomach, her vision narrowing to pinholes.

Panic attack, she tried to say, but terror stole her voice as she hyperventilated.

"Look me in the eyes!" demanded Greco. "Look me in the eyes and tell me why you killed them!"

She heard the words but didn't register them, her tight lungs staunchly refusing to accept the desperate gasps of air she frantically inhaled.

Stop, stop, stop.

She laid her forehead on the table, pressing it against the shallow puddle of spilt water, and closed her eyes, shutting out the men, the voices, shutting it *all* out.

Someone yanked her head up by her hair and screamed in her face, but her brain filtered the muffled shouts. Rough fingers pressed against her skin, opening her eyes, dragging the lids up. She saw their faces contorted with anger, bellowing silent accusations.

I want to die, she thought.

One of the men splashed water on her face.

I hate it here.

What would come next? Court? They would never believe her story. Would she go to prison? The idea appalled her, terrified her. She wouldn't manage. She *couldn't* manage.

And as the policemen held her eyes open and bellowed accusations, convinced she was a psychotic murderer, she realised beyond doubt that she no longer wished to be part of this awful, horrible world.

PC Laura Gill tapped her pen against the counter and waited for her shift to finish. It was Tuesday night, and the station had been busy all evening. They were currently in a lull, but she was convinced things would kick off again in a few minutes, right before she was due to clock out for the night. It was always the way.

"Must be a full moon," said PC Gordon. He was too close, and she could smell his rank body odour.

"What?"

"All the crazies are out. Moon drives 'em wild."

She nodded, eager to return to tapping her pen and watching the clock. Gordon made her feel uneasy. Not only did he smell bad, but he was always trying to peek at her arse.

"Something to do with psychic energies," Gordon continued.

"Is that a fact," she sighed, then worried he would misinterpret her disinterested sarcasm as a question. True to form, he did.

"Aye. Read it online. Moon affects everything, but especially loonies. Oh, and bears."

"Bears?"

"Bears. They cannae stop shagging when the moon's full."

Seven minutes to go. "Fascinating."

"Aye. The moon's fucking mental, eh?"

"Sure is," she said, willing the glass doors to remain closed for seven short minutes. She looked at the reflection of her own bored face, and saw PC Gordon standing behind her, his head tilted down and staring at her bum.

She turned and caught him. "Would you stop, please?"

"Stop what?"

Christ, she couldn't be bothered. She wanted to get home, take a bath, watch an episode of *Brooklyn Nine-Nine*, and go to bed. Only six minutes remained until she could make that happen.

"Aye, the moon does funny things to people," said Gordon, somehow still talking about the fucking moon. "You women have to be careful out there."

She side-eyed him. "Because of bears?"

"Because of the loonies. You know," he said, as if he hadn't been planning this all evening, "I'm finishing soon as well. Want me to walk you home? We can grab a drink on the way, if you like. Or dinner? Have you had—"

"Someone's coming," she said, gazing through the glass doors. A man approached through the car park, and she watched him, unable to work out how close he was. Judging by his size, he looked like he was only a few metres away, but the streetlamps that illuminated him were further back. It was an optical illusion, she told herself.

"Typical," said Gordon. "So anyway, you want to grab that drink?"

"Sure," said Gill, only half-listening.

"Really? Oh, wow, okay. I, uh... where do you wanna go?"

The man advanced on the station, slipping from the glare of the lamps and cloaking himself in shadow, before the next set illuminated him again. He wore all black, and his round, white face absorbed the lamplight, making it glow.

"Look at this guy," she said, a hint of awe in her voice. He was big. No, huge. *Massive*.

"Shit," chuckled Gordon, following her gaze. "Check out his face. There's your full moon." He stepped out from behind the counter. "Anyway, I'm gonna pop to the loo, then I'm done for the night. I'll, uh, wait for you out back, aye?"

"Stay a minute," she said, as the man outside stalked unhurriedly towards the station. He held something in both hands. A wooden pole, like a broom, or...

He walked into the light, and she saw exactly what it was.

A sledgehammer.

"Get help," she said. She looked around the front desk area. There were three people waiting; a businessman who had been mugged, and a mother and her teenage son. All three stared at their mobile phones, oblivious to the world around them. Should she evacuate?

"Don't worry," said Gordon, puffing himself up like a threatened cat. "I got this." He walked to the doors and waited before them, his arms crossed.

"I think we should get backup," said Gill, the tapping of her pen intensifying.

The man neared. One hand released the sledgehammer, and it trailed behind him, scraping across the concrete.

PC Gill turned her attention to the three people waiting. "Excuse me," she said. They ignored her, wrapped up in their phones. Only PC Gordon was paying attention, and then the big man outside reached the doors, hunching over and walking straight through the glass without stopping. The shards crunched beneath his heavy boots, and when he raised his lumpy, misshapen head, PC Gill got her first good look at him.

The pen slipped from her fingers.

"Good god," she said. "What the fuck is *that?*"

33

PC Gordon reacted quickly.

Drawing his police-issue baton, he charged, striking the intruder across the forearm. The big man didn't react. His head swivelled towards Gordon, the sledgehammer following at such devastating force that it ploughed through the officer's skull.

PC Gill stood immobile behind her desk. She reached for the alarm button, missing it the first time, then the second, and managing only on her third try. A siren blared throughout the station, and when she looked up, the big man's head had turned in her direction. He walked forwards, each mighty step causing the desk to rumble. The soft remains of PC Gordon were caught on the end of the sledgehammer, and they squelched along the floor like a gore-drenched mop as the man dragged the bludgeoning instrument behind him.

Gill wanted to run, but she couldn't comprehend the horror before her. She was new to the force, only six months into the job, and Gordon was the first real-life death she had ever witnessed. She stared up into the nightmare pools where the man's eyes should be, and as the shrill alarm blared, the people in the waiting area ran screaming through the broken door. The woman fell, and her teenage son helped her to her feet, the pair escaping into the night. Gill watched them leave, teardrops forming in the corners of her eyes.

"Can... can I help you?"

The giant freak wore a long, black leather garment. He reached one hand inside, then removed it, clutching sheaves of loose papers. Gill jumped as he slammed them onto the desk and slid them towards her. She picked one up. Her hand trembled so violently that she struggled to read the fine print, but at the top was the word MISSING, and beneath it, a photo of an intense-looking toddler. The man stood, motionless. What did he want? Was he reporting a missing person? She looked again, gripping the paper with both hands, scrunching the edges in her terrified grip.

> Rebecca Tremayne, last seen on the
> twenty-sixth of December, 1984.

That was thirty years ago. Shit, no, *forty*. She didn't know what to do, or what to say, but she *did* know that if she didn't say something, she was going to join PC Gordon on the business end of the sledgehammer.

Gill jerked her thumb over her shoulder. "That way," she said.

The big man regarded her, then stomped past the desk to the swing doors that led into the station. He bashed his way through, and by the time they swung shut, and the desperate screams of dying men and women began in earnest, Gill had left the building through the shattered glass doors, and was already composing her letter of resignation in her head.

~

What now? thought Becky, as the siren erupted from a speaker above the door. What new and terrible hell was this? Hadn't they tortured her enough?

Greco released her, turning to his partner and sharing a conspiratorial glance. He said something to her, his words drowned out by the noise, and the two men hastily left the room.

Becky's face stung from Greco's probing fingers, and she shut her eyes tight, unable to block out the alarm. It seemed to be getting louder, like an orchestra building to an atonal crescendo. Was there a fire? She may be a murder suspect, but they couldn't abandon her in this barren room to die. She tugged on the cuffs, attempting to slide them over her thumb.

No use.

As the door closed, she saw more officers racing by. Something was happening, some emergency, like a terrorist attack, or... or...

He's coming.

No. No way, no fucking way.

He's coming for you.

It wasn't possible. He couldn't find her. Not here, not in the safety of a police station.

It's you he wants.

She rattled her handcuffs uselessly.

It's you he's always wanted.

~

Inspector Carlson had been munching reheated pepperoni pizza in the break room when the alarm sounded, pizza that now decorated the front of his otherwise pristine white shirt after the piercing siren caught him unawares.

He staggered from the break room, melted cheese staining the crisp white cotton, and two officers racing by almost knocked him down in their haste. "What's going on?" he shouted after them. They kept running, oblivious to his enquiry. More officers charged down the hallway, and Carlson — who had always been a follower rather than a leader — figured he should probably run in the same direction.

The officers sprinted around the corner. Not wishing the younger men and women to show him up, Carlson broke into a jog. "Hey, where are you going?" His legs were tired, and he was still hungover from the weekend. "Guys, wait up!"

He was almost at the end of the corridor when one of the officers reappeared. The woman hurtled backwards as if shot from a cannon, smacking hard against the wall. Carlson ran to her. A trail of blood led from a crack in the wall where her skull had struck, all the way down to where she now sat. He looked into her glazed eyes, checking for signs of concussion, before her head drooped forwards, leaving a juicy red stain on the cracked plaster.

She was dead.

Were they under attack? A siege from a local Edinburgh gang? He turned and looked down the corridor.

"Holy mother of god," he whispered.

A man stood there, filling the space like an escaped rhinoceros. A dead cop lay at his feet, and the big man pummelled the officer's chest with a sledgehammer. Blood erupted with each blow, reminding Carlson of the time his infant son had banged his fist off the table in McDonalds and accidentally burst a ketchup sachet. The thick fluid coated the walls and the lights, turning the interior into a sinister crimson hell. The killer looked at him, and without hesitation, raised the sledgehammer and threw it. It spun through the air like an axe, end over end, and Carlson dodged sideways as the mighty hammer whirled past him and embedded itself in the wall above the dead female officer.

He needed to get to the armoury. Scottish police officers didn't carry guns, but the bigger stations had armouries for emergency situations, and if this wasn't an emergency, then what the fuck was?

He ran for the basement, and though he couldn't *hear* the man over the alarm, he felt the ground vibrate with each pounding footstep. There were two officers ahead, running towards him. Carlson waved his hands, shrieking for them to turn back, but the men didn't hear. He grabbed the second officer, an older man he recognised as Sergeant Durning, and spun him around.

"The armoury!" he shouted, glancing over his shoulder as the big man rounded the corner, colliding with the second officer. Carlson stared in disbelief as the moon-faced murderer punched his fist through the young man's stomach, emerging triumphantly from the other side clutching the officer's spine.

Carlson spun Sergeant Durning to face him. *"The armoury!"* he screamed again. Durning nodded, his face grim, and together the men ran for the nearest staircase. They had a full arsenal of pistols, shotguns, and machine guns down there, and even a stash of C4 explosives.

Enough to start a war... or to end one.

On the way, they corralled every officer they found,

leading the small army down the stairs to the basement. At the bottom, they burst through the doors and passed the toilets, the lockers, the evidence room, until finally, at the far end of—

Wait a minute.

Carlson slipped to the back of the pack, allowing Durning to lead the dozen-or-so officers to the locked weaponry storage while he doubled back on himself, racing to the evidence room. He kicked open the door, his hangover a distant memory, and entered the evidence room. The technician rose from his seat, cupping his hands around his mouth.

"Quite an entrance" he shouted over the alarm. "What's happening out there?"

Carlson had no time to explain. "Unlock the cage, I need to get in!"

The technician gawped at him. "What, now? You'll need authorisation from—"

He grabbed the man by his lapels and slammed him against the wall. "Hurry! *He's killing everyone!*"

The technician fumbled in his pocket for the keys and handed them to Carlson, who snatched them up and raced to the sealed cage, where years-worth of evidence was safely stored.

He only prayed he could find what he was looking for in time.

34

The handcuff chain rasped against the metal bar as Becky dug her heels into the floor and pulled. The cuffs tore the top layers of her skin, and blood oozed onto the table. She was going nowhere.

Outside the interrogation room, people screamed, shouted, barked orders, while the siren wailed at maximum volume, drowning out their panicked cries.

It was *her* Tommy wanted, not them. Though when she had told her interrogators about him, they had laughed at her. In a grotesque way, it felt like her school days all over again.

A gifted child, her primary teachers had called her. *Such an aptitude for the English language. If only she could have more confidence and learn to project her voice.*

She had scraped by, but secondary school was a different matter. The constant changing of classes, the ringing of the bell just as she was settling down in a new environment, and the unexplained social conventions that other teenagers seemed to intuitively understand. It was like everyone on the planet had been given a secret social rulebook at a young age, while hers had been printed in Chinese due to some cosmic administrative balls-up. She had tried to blend into the background, losing herself in books and music, desperate not to be noticed, but her peers had known something was different about her, and children could be so fucking cruel.

Even as an adult, when she was supposed to have some semblance of control over her life, she found herself here, in a police station, wanted for murders she hadn't committed, aware they would, inevitably, use her own brain against her. She wasn't the 'useful' type of autistic person seen in Hollywood movies; a savant genius who performed complicated mathematical equations in her head, or who could hack into the Pentagon on a whim. No, she came armed with a truckload of facts about Jason Statham and penguins, and the ability to recite every word of the *Lord of the Rings* films — theatrical *and* extended versions — by heart.

The world had no use for her.

Not for the first time in her life, Becky wondered if death was the best way out. Though she had never *seriously* contemplated suicide, the idea of it rarely left her mind. It was an obsession, a game she played late at night, picturing her funeral, with Flora and John the sole mourners. Though now, she imagined them sneaking off mid-service for a cheeky shag in the chapel toilet. Well, the joke was on her, because her only two mourners were dead, and any moment now, their killer would enter the room and dispose of her too.

Life had a funny way of circling back.

She gave up on the handcuffs and looked at her bleeding wrists. Her thumb was the problem. Could she bite it off?

No, that was stupid. She may be able to crunch through skin, cartilage, and muscle, but not bone. Dislocation? Would *that* work?

"Code red, code red!" someone yelled as they ran past the door.

Becky stared at her hand. How best to dislocate a thumb? The cuffs prevented her from raising her hand high and slamming it onto the table, so she tried using her left hand to squeeze the knuckle of her right thumb.

No use. She had neither the strength nor the willpower.

An idea came to her. She placed her hand on the table like she was performing a karate chop, with her thumb at a slight angle.

"Okay," she whispered, then, before she had a chance to change her mind, she rammed her head onto her hand, her forehead striking her knuckle. It hurt, and she yelped in pain, but not *enough* pain. More force was required. She tried again, harder this time. Something clicked, and her head struck the metal table. Too fired up to feel groggy, she inspected her thumb.

Not dislocated.

"Fuck!" she screamed.

Tommy was close. Somehow, she knew. He was coming to get her.

And he would kill her.

It's you he wants. It's you he's always wanted.

"Why?" she asked, and headbutted her thumb again. "Why me?" Once more. Her head ached, but she refused to give up. Again and again, harder each time, until she heard a crack and thought her skull had broken. The white-hot pain in her hand told her otherwise. Success! Agonising success!

She snapped her dislocated thumb to the side and

hauled her arm backwards, making it further through the handcuffs than before… but not far enough.

Pressing her feet against the table legs, she pulled, drawing not on reserves of strength, but of sheer, blind panic. The sharp edges of the cuffs dug wickedly into her skin, slicing deep, peeling her hand like an orange. Glistening muscle throbbed under the crude fluorescent glow.

Come on, come on!

With a wet tearing sound, a chunk of skin came loose, and her hand slipped free from the cuff. She staggered to the wall, her entire arm throbbing in anguished torment, the cuffs swinging back and forth from her left wrist like a noose in the wind.

Free. She was free. So what now?

One thing was for sure. She couldn't stay here.

Becky ran for the door, her injured hand tucked into her armpit. She grasped the handle, pressed it down, and…

"No," she groaned. *"No!"*

Locked.

…Keep the door locked night and day…

The fucking door was locked.

She stepped back, bumping up against the table, as menacing footsteps, heavy and ponderous, drew closer. They paused outside the door.

The handle moved.

Click.

She glanced around for a way to defend herself, for a place to hide. Three chairs and a table. That was it. Fuck! She looked at her damaged hand, at the rapidly swelling joints and the early stages of a dark purple bruise, and at the bloody, exposed muscle. She wouldn't be able to *lift* one of the chairs without two working thumbs, never mind fight Tommy off with one.

The door opened, and Becky turned towards it. There, squeezing through the doorway, his gaping mouth locked in a silent, shrieking spiral, was Rotten Tommy. He had found her.

And this time, there would be no escape.

35

Thin cracks shot along the wall as Tommy forced his way inside. Once through, his enormous physique concealed the doorway like a lunar eclipse.

This is it, thought Becky. *The end.*

There was nowhere left to go. "What do you want?" she yelled at the colossal brute. "What do you fucking want from me?"

Tommy's clothes were drenched in blood. It coated his white face, his hands, *everything.*

She retreated to the farthest corner of the room, pressing up against the cold, bare walls as Tommy took a step closer. "Get it over with," she said, sliding down into a crouch, the power in her limbs draining fast.

He reached for his smock and unsnapped one of the leather straps that held it shut. Suddenly, a new terror rocked Becky, one she couldn't have fathomed in her wildest nightmares. Was he undressing?

No, she mouthed, searching for a way out.

He unfastened another strap, and the garment sagged open, exposing the semi-transparent skin of his chest.

Crimson veins swarmed beneath the layers, beyond which pulsed a vast, black heart. He reached inside his smock and took two thunderous steps closer. She gazed up at her soon-to-be murderer, at the revolting flesh of the monster who had taken her mother, and who had left a trail of carnage across the country in his mad search for *her,* his intended victim.

Tommy removed his hand from his clothing and held his fist out to her. The fingers uncurled like a spider waking from a dream, and when he twisted his wrist, something soft fell from his grasp, landing in front of Becky.

She looked at the item with incredulous eyes, waiting for Tommy to kill her, to crush her, to rend her limb-from-limb. When he didn't move, she reached out and grabbed his gift.

"Grumpus," she said, cradling her favourite cuddly penguin. She brushed his plush fur against her cheek, knotting his flippers through her fingers. "You brought him back to me."

Tommy loomed over her, his face an obscure frozen horror, and extended his hand. What did he want? Was he—

"He's in here!" cried a woman.

Becky looked past Tommy, to the female officer in the doorway, a gun swaying in her nervous hands. The officer noticed Becky, and turned the barrel on her.

"Don't move," she said, then half-leaned out the door. *"Hey! Anybody there? They're in interrogation room one!"*

"Please," said Becky, as she battled against exhaustion and gravity to force herself to stand. "Don't shoot." She shuffled away from the officer, away from Tommy, as the woman tracked her with the gun. She shouted something, yet while Becky saw the officer's lips move, she heard nothing but a high-pitched whine in her eardrums.

"I'm innocent," she said, stepping closer. "I didn't kill anybody. You have to believe—"

The officer aimed low and squeezed the trigger. Becky screamed as a bullet entered her leg with a wet pop. A spray of blood fountained from her thigh as she dropped to the floor. The pain was excruciating, momentarily overriding her other agonies. Pressing one hand over the wound, she felt the hot blood spurting against her palm. Why? Why had the woman perceived her as a threat? Why had she opened fire?

Why, why, *why?*

What the fuck was wrong with people? Why did they live to hurt, to maim, to kill? Theirs was a world of terror and bloodshed, where only the strong and the rich prevailed, while the weak and the poor and the vulnerable were seen as useless, less than nothing, expendable.

Expendable...

Expendable... just like the Jason Statham movie.

Lying on the interrogation room floor in a pool of blood — her *own* blood — Becky couldn't help but wonder what Jason Statham would do in a situation like this. Frank Martin from *The Transporter* series would never beg for his life. *Crank's* Chev Chelios wouldn't suffer this indignity, this humiliation. And Luke Wright in *Safe* would certainly have a quip stored away for times like these.

But Statham's characters didn't always work alone. From *The Expendables* to the *Fast and the Furious* saga, and from *Killer Elite* to *The Italian Job,* not even The Best Shaped Head in Hollywood could always manage by himself.

Sometimes, even Jason Statham needed a friend.

She looked to Tommy, his hand still outstretched, and said, "Take me away from here."

Tommy watched her. He nodded once, then spun on the police officer with a speed that belied his size.

"Stop!" the officer said, her voice drained of authority. "Or I'll—"

She never got a chance to finish. Tommy lunged at the woman, grabbing her by the throat and lifting her. Her legs kicked at thin air, and she pulled the trigger, the shots reverberating throughout the cramped room. Bullets thumped into Tommy, but the big man didn't flinch. He swung the officer around and headed towards the metal table, holding her inches from the sharp-angled corner. With a surge of maniac strength, he rammed the woman's face forwards. The corner ruptured her nose, splitting the juicy organ in two. He forced her onwards with both hands, the woman's skull cracking, floods of scarlet blood gushing from her newly bisected face, shards of fractured skull piercing her skin with jagged points that burst through the flesh like miniature tectonic plates shifting beneath the Earth.

The officer slumped to the ground.

We're all just bags of meat, thought Becky. *Useless meat suits blundering our way through life, trying to survive.*

And sometimes, surviving was enough.

Becky looked at her leg, where her jeans were turning a dark, angry red. A shadow fell across her, offering a welcome respite from the headache-inducing lights, and without thinking, she reached up and took Tommy's hand. He raised her to her feet.

"Thank you," she said, and for the first time in many years, she felt an unfamiliar surge inside her head, a strange rushing sensation towards her eyeballs. Tears forced their way out and rolled down her cheeks.

Everyone she knew was dead, and the police — hell, the whole country — thought *she* was the killer. They would not allow her to leave here alive. From the day of her birth, the world had refused to accept her, and that was okay.

She didn't want to be here anyway.

Tommy placed his arm around her waist and helped her to the door. She had no choice but to follow him. They were in this together now. He was all she had left. The police would not differentiate between them, for their orders would be simple.

Shoot on sight, and shoot to kill.

Becky stooped and picked up the female officer's discarded pistol. It was heavy, the grip satisfyingly tactile.

Through the door, she heard more shouts, more orders, the police preparing themselves for the final onslaught. She readied the gun in her hand, craning her neck to look up at Tommy.

"Come on," she said, her cheeks wet with welcome tears. She had forgotten how good it felt to cry. "Let's go home."

36

As Tommy left the interrogation room and emerged in the corridor, raucous gunfire erupted, turning the narrow space into a miniature war zone. Becky sheltered behind him, using his massive bulk for balance and protection. In one hand, she held the police officer's gun, and in the other, Grumpus the penguin. She didn't want to fire the weapon, not when she had lived her life trying never to hurt anyone. But *they* had shot her first, and if it came down to it... she would do what she must to live.

The deafening cacophony of gunfire continued, some bullets striking Tommy, some slamming into the walls, others ricocheting off metal pipes that snaked along the ceiling. Tommy let nothing faze him. He lurched forwards, shielding Becky from harm as she limped after him, grimacing in pain that flared from the sizzling circle in her thigh.

"Basement floor, send backup!" shouted a gruff officer between gunshots.

They advanced on the police, the noise lessening as the officers expended their ammunition. Becky dared to peek out from behind Tommy, and saw three crouching men armed with pistols. A fourth officer, this one wielding a shotgun, stood over them. He fired, and Tommy took the blast to his chest.

"Aim for the head!" he commanded. The men fired, stray bullets thudding into the walls in puffs of curling white smoke, and then Tommy was on them. Becky heard bones breaking, flesh tearing, and the sickening crunch of skulls cracking. Agonised wails filled the air, grown men shrieking like children.

Something whizzed past her ear.

A bullet.

It struck Tommy, burying into his back. Down the corridor, an officer aimed a gun at her. She raised her own pistol in response.

"Stop shooting!" she yelled. "I don't want to—"

Grumpus exploded in her hand. The bullet passed through his body, and white stuffing burst like fluffy entrails from holes ringed with black scorch marks.

Without thinking, Becky returned fire.

Her aim was true.

The officer's head rocked back, a third eye opening above his nose, blood belching from the wound and cascading in rivers down his astounded face.

Becky stared at the weapon in horror and sadness. She clutched the injured Grumpus to her chest, pressing his stuffing in with her thumb as Tommy's hand closed over her forearm and pulled her further down the corridor. They turned the corner, where more officers waited. The moment they saw Tommy, they opened fire.

There was too much noise, too much light.

The intense gunfire rocked Tommy. He stumbled backwards, and for the first time, Becky wondered if he could die.

"We have to find another way out!" she shouted, but Tommy was one step ahead. He raised his fists and thrust them into the ceiling. She scrambled out of the way as the paint cracked, plaster and concrete shrieking as the upstairs floor crumbled. With one forceful pull, Tommy tore the ceiling down, chunks of masonry — and one rather unfortunate police officer — crashing to the ground. Tommy rose to his full height, searching through the hole, then lifted Becky and deposited her on the floor above. To a chorus of mindless gunshots, he clambered up after her.

They traversed the ground floor, the ever-present siren blaring over hidden speakers, and emerged in a large open-plan office space, surrounded by dozens of cubicles filled with computer screens and phones and plastic trays groaning with paperwork. She followed Tommy between the desks.

He was bleeding heavily. It poured from him, leaving a thick trail along the floor.

"Are you okay?"

He didn't answer. She doubted he could.

Boom!

A ferocious roar erupted. Tommy stumbled backwards, almost falling, as another officer appeared from behind a desk, this one cradling a shotgun. Jesus, there were too many of them! The cop kept firing as he advanced on Tommy, each blast coming close to knocking the big man off-balance. Becky recognised the officer.

It was that bastard interrogator, Fuller. And if *he* was here, she wondered if his partner was—

"Ooof!"

A heavy body slammed into her.

"I got you, bitch!" snarled Greco, spit flying from his lips as he wrestled her to the ground. She tried to angle the gun towards his head, but Greco swatted her hand away. Out of desperation, she brought her knee up sharply between his legs, relishing the satisfying crunch of his testicles. Greco's jaw dropped, and Becky pressed the gun against his belly and fired. The bastard howled in agony, and she used the opportunity to shove him away and roll out from under him.

She glanced at Tommy as she scrambled to her feet. The big man had dropped to one knee. Rivers of blood gushed in unceasing torrents from his brutalised torso, as Fuller — who had evidently run out of shells — battered him around the head with the empty shotgun.

Becky turned back to Greco, who lumbered after her, clutching his stomach to staunch the flow of blood. "I don't have time for this!" she cried, and raised the pistol, aiming at his head. "Just leave me alone!" She closed her eyes and pulled the trigger, flinching at the harsh report. When she opened them, Greco lay twitching on the floor.

She had no time to watch him die. Tommy was on his knees, his blank eyes almost level with Fuller's, who was sliding fresh shells into his shotgun. Tommy swayed like a giant redwood in a hurricane, as Fuller put the last shell in place and pumped the shotgun. He pressed the barrel to Tommy's head, which wept blood from splits and cracks in his malleable dome.

"Hey!" screamed Becky, and Fuller looked at her, a splenetic grimace plastered to his cruel face. "Catch, you fucker!"

She hurled an object at the officer, and Fuller, instinctively, dropped the shotgun and raised both hands to catch it. The fearful expression he wore suggested the expectation of a grenade, or some other explosive device. When

Grumpus the plush penguin landed in his grasping hands, he stared at the cuddly friend for a couple of seconds, trying to figure out what the hell had just happened, and by the time he realised his mistake, Becky had thrown herself to the floor, sliding along the trail of blood towards the discarded shotgun. She snatched it, spun onto her back, and came to a stop between Fuller's legs, the barrel aimed directly between them.

It was what Jason Statham would have done.

Fuller had just enough time to say, "Oh, *fuck*," before she pulled the trigger.

The interrogator opened up like a flower in bloom, his upper half disintegrating in a savage explosion of blood and vital organs. Soggy intestines smacked against the walls and the desks, as the two legs, which had parted like a wishbone, toppled to either side.

Grumpus landed next to Becky, his once-white fur now a deep red that would *never* come out in the wash. She tried to stand, but the adrenaline that had sustained her, that had snapped her out of her stress-imposed fatigue, was wearing off. The pain returned, grievous pain that blazed through her leg and prevented her from *standing,* never mind walking.

"Tommy," she croaked, as she dragged herself across the blood-slicked floor. His clothes — and skin — were mostly gone. Stringy, black tapeworms squirmed from between slabs of doughy flesh, and his face was a revolting, punctured softness drenched in oozing blood.

"Can you make it?"

Tommy lumbered to his feet, chunks of sour muscle sliding from cracked, greying bones. With aching slowness, he hooked his thumbs into his head and rotated them to create two eye-like craters, before carving a crooked smile onto his pulped face.

"So what now?" asked Becky.

"Now..." came a voice from behind her, *"you die."*

"Oh, *fuck off*," she muttered. Not another policeman? She was exhausted, and pain wracked her body. Hell, she had a bullet lodged in her thigh. The shotgun was out of reach, but Tommy was already heading past her to deal with the newcomer. Like all the rest, the dumb bastard didn't stand a chance. Why didn't they just give up?

She rolled over and looked in the officer's direction. Her vision was blurred, and she blinked hard, squinting at the man.

Her eyes widened.

"Oh, *come on,*" she said, as she realised what the absolute fucking *psychopath* was carrying.

37

At last, Carlson had them in his sights. Tracking the fugitives had been the simple part, for the pair of cop-killers left a trail of devastation in their bloody wake. Sure, he had spent too long searching the evidence room, but it would all be worth it now.

The rocket launcher rested on his shoulder, the giant firmly in the firing line. He would annihilate the monster and his female companion for what they had done to his station. To his *friends*. And if he died too? Then so be it. At least he would die a hero.

God, he remembered the day they discovered the anti-aircraft device during a raid on a supposed drug den in Niddrie, one of Edinburgh's most crime-ridden areas. He and several colleagues had stormed the building at five in the morning, breaking in unannounced and working their way through the flat on an anonymous tip-off. They found few drugs — pot and ketamine don't count for much — but the real prize was concealed beneath the floorboards. Shotguns, assault rifles, even a box of hand grenades; a stash of weapons the likes of which Carlson had never seen. There was enough firepower to bring a small country to its knees, and even more astonishingly, the cache had been hidden beneath a baby's crib.

And when Carlson had found the secret compartment in the wardrobe, and pulled forth the fucking *rocket launcher,* no one present could quite believe their eyes. The idea of a destructive weapon like this falling into the wrong hands had chilled him at the time, but now it was going to be put to good use.

"Divine retribution," he said, and smiled.

"Don't do it," the woman begged. She was a fucking mess. Bleeding heavily, her clothes torn, and cuddling a stuffed animal, he wondered how much involvement she had in this depraved murder spree. Then he remembered she had been found in a car with the remains of Detective Constable Larkin, manic and covered in his blood.

"Fuck you both," he said, and flipped down the switch to fire the rocket.

∼

So this is how it ends, she thought.

Not with a whimper, but with a bang. A *big* fucking bang.

Becky could do nothing. Even if she wanted to, her limbs no longer responded, her entire body a sick animal ready to be put out of its misery. She watched the policeman gaze through the sights and curl his finger around the trigger. In a way, she was glad. Death was preferable to going to jail, which would result in the same thing, albeit slower and more painfully. She looked at Tommy, still unsure what he wanted, or why he had chosen her. But that didn't matter either. It was simply one more mystery she would never understand in a lifetime of perpetual bafflement. And anyway, facing death head-on was a quite exciting. What if there was some sort of afterlife, or—

The rocket fired.

38

Fire.

Fire everywhere.

Her hair was burning. Her clothes and skin, too.

Everything hurt. Every single tiny molecule of her body screamed in wretched despair.

She couldn't see, she couldn't breathe.

God, the pain! And to be so aware throughout... that was the worst part.

This never happened to Jason Statham, she thought, and laughed as the fire hungrily consumed her.

Then she felt him.

Tommy, crawling towards her, climbing atop her and using his body to smother the flames.

Above, the roof cracked. The whole station was going to come down soon.

The whole station.

The whole world.

Soon, so soon, it would all be over.

At fucking last.

PART IV

6 MONTHS LATER

keep the dooR locked night and day, keep the dOor locked nighT and day, keep ThE door locked Night and day, keep the dooR locked night and day, keep the dOor locked nighT and day, keep The door locked night and day, keEp the door locked Night and day, keep the dooR locked night and day, keep the doOr locked nighT and day, keep the door locked nighT and day, kEep the door locked Night and day, keep the dooR locked night and day, keep the dOor locked nighT and day, keep The door lockEd Night and day, so

39

Serge Barron sat in front of his computer screen wearing nothing but his socks and underpants. The Wi-Fi was playing up again, and he couldn't even load Reddit, never mind any of his favourite porn sites.

Horny and frustrated, he opened his video folder and scrolled through the thumbnails. It was mostly torrented wrestling pay-per-views, alongside a bunch of films, but nothing he was in the mood for on a lonely Tuesday night.

An odd title caught his eye in the endless scrolling list.

Rumplejack.

What the fuck was that? He couldn't recall downloading it. Was it porn? He opened the file, excited to find out. As the opening credits played, a lone voice sang.

"Let's go back,
To Rumplejack,
We've been away too long."

Well, it wasn't porn, but a smile spread across Serge's lips as he remembered the source of the video. Andy had sent it to him the night he died, claiming it was a piece of lost media that would make for an excellent episode of their YouTube series. Serge had paid little attention at the time, because Andy was notorious for over-hyping things. Then, when his friend had been murdered by a disgruntled customer, Serge had laid *Land of the Lost Media* to rest with one final tribute episode, and moved on with his life.

"Your friends await,
So don't be late,
To help them sing this song."

He missed it, though. The buzz of seeking out the unseen, of unravelling enigmas. Not only that, but the fun of recording, and of the natural dopamine high from the inevitable likes and comments. Perhaps, if this content was as rare as Andy had promised, he could resurrect the show? This time, he would hire a good-looking babe with big bazongas to co-host, and add some much-needed sex appeal.

It was what Andy would have wanted.

The credits finished, and the image cut to a shot of a lighthouse on a windswept Scottish coastline. A woman limped into frame. Her face was burnt, and what few strands of hair remained on her head fluttered ethereally in the wind.

"Like fucking Freddy Krueger on kids TV," said Serge. He chuckled in admiration. "That's *brilliantly* fucked up. Andy, my man, you might've been onto something here."

Serge sat back, tucked his junk into his undies, and watched the episode unfold, as the burnt woman—

∼

—neared her home, struggling against a howling gale that battered her face.

As usual, her leg throbbed. She supposed she would get used to it. And anyway, the grocery shop was open all day and night, and well-stocked with free painkillers. Tramadol, Codeine, Oxycodone... whatever she needed to dull the pain.

Becky had lived in the lighthouse for six months now, and — as she had always known she would — she loved it.

The first few weeks had been hard. Adjusting to a new life and new surroundings, while finding and perfecting her routines, had taken a toll. Now, though, she felt truly settled.

After Tommy's burial, and the subsequent three day long town celebration, the other residents had vanished. It happened overnight. Even the dead bodies that littered the place simply... *evaporated,* or something. Becky liked to think the townspeople were free of whatever strange curse had kept them prisoner, but honestly? She didn't know for sure. Only The Sausage King did, and he refused to explain until she brought him sausages.

He was a very demanding monarch, especially for a king who was so small, and whose tail was so curly, and whose little button nose was so black and shiny. And while she missed Grumpus, The Sausage King was a good friend. Anyway, it was her fault Grumpus was no longer around. She had buried the penguin with Tommy, so that the big man would always have a friend by his side. It was the least she could do.

She smiled to herself and looked into her shopping bag, which was full to the brim with strings of sausages. Tonight, The Sausage King would feast like the royalty he was, and tell her the whole sordid saga. She was sure of it.

It was getting late, and night fell suddenly in Rumplejack, so she hobbled onwards to the lighthouse, to her *home,* pausing only once to look over her shoulder, convinced someone was watching.

~

"Not exactly high-octane stuff," said Serge. He left the video playing as he retrieved a beer from the fridge. When he returned, the woman was limping her way up a set of stone stairs. Serge shook his head. "What the *fuck* is going on?"

~

Becky reached the lamp room and laid her bag on the floor. God, that was the one thing she'd never considered about living in a lighthouse; the dreaded stairs and ladders. Still, the journey kept her active, and that was important.

The Sausage King lay flat and lifeless on the table, and before waking him, she opened the door and carried a foldaway chair onto the gallery. She placed her bag next to it, then slipped The Sausage King onto her left hand. Her right hand had never been the same since freeing herself from the handcuffs in the police station. Mind you, neither had her leg. One time, The Sausage King had tried to dig the bullet out of her thigh using a scalpel, but his tiny paws lacked dexterity, and he ended up slicing open a few veins instead. How they had laughed!

After that fiasco, they left the bullet alone as a reminder of her past, of a life spent trying to survive in a world that wasn't built with her in mind.

"Hello," said The Sausage King. He stretched his paws, and Becky carried him outside to the lighthouse gallery. The cool breeze ruffled his fur, and, together, they sat as the waves battered the rocks far below, and the rapidly setting sun turned the frothing sea blood red.

Becky rested her tired legs on the barrier. "You got any plans tonight?"

The Sausage King gazed out to sea. "Well, it's Saturday. I thought we might go to the discotheque?"

She smiled at the silly dog. "It's *Tuesday,* Sausage King. And you know I don't like the disco."

"Tuesday? Why, that's even better! We'll have the whole place to ourselves."

"We have the whole of *Rumplejack* to ourselves."

"True. But I'd like to go to the discotheque. I'm in a dancing mood."

Becky leaned back in the chair. It had been decades since she last went out dancing. She had tried it in her teens, but the crowds of people and the loud music and the bass that rumbled her insides had given her a panic attack. Her friends had found her hours later, sitting outside with her head in her hands. Sure, it would be only her and The Sausage King in Rumplejack's sole nightclub, but that didn't alter the fact she didn't know *how* to dance.

"Tell me about Tommy," she said, and she felt the puppet droop on her hand.

"I don't think that's wise. Let him rest in peace. The sooner Rumplejack moves on from Tommy's wicked reign, the better."

"But I need to know," urged Becky. "It's important."

"What, precisely, do you *need* to know?"

For a glorified glove, he could be pretty damn patronising.

"Everything," said Becky. "Who *was* Tommy? Where did he come from? Why did he take my mother? What did he want with me? Why isn't Rumplejack on any map? For that matter, who the hell is the Rylak Corporation, and why do they bring me food and drink and supplies once a week?"

The Sausage King snorted. "You think knowing all that will make a difference? Does it change what happened, or how you feel? Sometimes, in life, there are no explanations. Things just... are."

Annoyed, she shook her head. "But I've gone my whole life not understanding, or knowing why something happened, or how to do things everyone else finds easy. I learned how to wash my hair and brush my teeth by watching movies. Shit," she smiled, "eighties action films taught me that I should spend most of my time in the shower soaping my breasts, so that's what I did until my ex-husband told me I had a problem."

The Sausage King laughed.

"He said it was weird," she continued, "but back then, he found my weirdness charming. Eventually, that changed." She turned to the puppet. "Please. If you know the answers to any of my questions, tell me."

"I'm sorry," he said, shaking his adorable round head. "That's the one thing I will never—"

"I brought you sausages."

"And I will tell you *anything* you wish to know."

"Thought so," she grinned, and scooped the first string of sausages from her bag. She dangled them above The Sausage King's slobbering, open mouth, and he greedily gobbled them up. Where the hell did they go? Ah, but that was a question for another time.

"Okay, you've had your sausages. Now, you promised."

"I'm well aware of my promises," he sighed. It was *such* an unusual feeling for your hand to sigh, and it always made Becky giggle. "I hope you're ready, my friend. It's a very long, and very upsetting story."

"I'm ready."

The Sausage King licked his nose, then began his epic tale.

"It all started many years ago, long before—"

∼

"Oh great, an exposition dump," said Serge. He skipped along the timeline. "Boo-o-o-o-o-o-oring."

The burnt-faced woman and the puppet were still talking. He clicked further along until the scene changed to a nightclub interior. A disco ball spun lazily from the ceiling, casting sparkling reflections over the empty dance floor. The dog puppet was visible in the background, sitting in the DJ booth on the hand of... a department store mannequin?

"Fucking weird-ass show," muttered Serge.

There was a knock at his door. He checked his phone and saw it was quarter to midnight. Who the hell was calling at this hour?

∼

Becky hovered awkwardly near the edge of the dance floor, a glass of lemonade in her hand. She sipped the drink through a straw as The Sausage King, behind the glass partition, bopped back and forth to Donna Summer's *Hot Stuff*.

Dance. Go dance.

Ah, she couldn't. It was embarrassing. She remembered how the walls in her sister's flat had been covered in prints with stupid slogans on them, like *Keep Calm and Drink Gin* and the dreaded *Live Laugh Love*. But the one that Becky hated the most was *Dance like nobody's watching*. She wasn't sure if it was because of the triteness of the slogan, or because she detected a hint of truth behind it. Why *couldn't* she dance like no one was watching? Especially at a time like this, when — with the exception of a glass-eyed puppet — literally no one *was* watching.

"That was Donna Summer," squeaked The Sausage King over the mic. "And she sure is hot stuff, am I right?" Becky thought he sounded like a local radio disc jockey. Alan Pugtridge, or something. "Now, here's one for you nineties kids. This song goes out to my good friend Becky, the only lady who I let put her hand up my backside. If this tune was fiction, it would be... *Pulp* fiction."

A guitar riff kicked in, and Becky smiled as *Disco 2000* by her favourite band Pulp came on. Her foot tapped along with the beat, and she glanced around the room. It was empty.

Should she...?

∽

The knocking continued. Serge tore his eyes from the screen, where the woman was nodding to the music. What he failed to understand was how a song from the nineties was playing in a video that supposedly came from the early eighties. Was the whole thing a spoof? A clever piece of retro fakery?

Knock knock knock.

"Jesus, I'm coming," said Serge. "Gimme a second." As the video played on, he stormed angrily to the door, sliding the chain into place before opening it. It was likely a tourist looking for the fuckin' Airbnb upstairs. They always got the wrong door.

"Do you know what time it—"

The door burst open, knocking him backwards.

Three men in black suits entered in single file.

"Who the fuck are you assholes?" Serge demanded. He was a big lad, and a practitioner of Brazilian martial art Capoeira. He could beat the shit out of—

"Uh," he gasped, wincing at a sharp pinch in his stomach. He looked from the smoking hole in his belly to the silenced pistol in the first man's hand, then collapsed onto his chair.

∽

Becky knew there was no one there, but fuck, why could she never quite shake the feeling someone was watching her?

She shuffled onto the dance floor and nodded her head from one side to the other. God, she adored this song. During her extreme Pulp phase, she could prattle on for hours at high school parties about the band, dispensing trivia and minutiae to an increasingly dwindling audience. She remembered talking to a boy she fancied, and trying to woo him by explaining that the fountain Jarvis Cocker mentioned in the chorus was the Goodwin Fountain in Sheffield City Centre, and that 'Deborah' was based on a real person. The boy had made his excuses and slipped upstairs to get a blowjob from Nelly Greengrass instead.

"Oh, well. Fuck him."

She swayed her body and took a deep breath.

That was her old life.

Everything was different now.

Here, in Rumplejack, she was allowed to exist.

She started to dance.

∽

"What do you want?" gasped Serge, blood leaking down his white underpants.

The men didn't answer. Two of them ransacked his room, opening drawers and tossing tapes and hard drives into a pile, while the third man stood by Serge, the hot barrel of the gun pressed against his temple.

"Where did you get this video?" asked the man who had shot him.

"What?"

"The video. Where did you get it?"

"A friend. A friend sent it. Please, don't—"

"Did you make any copies?"

"Huh? No, no, I just started watching it!"

"That video belongs to the Rylak Corporation. You're hoarding stolen property, did you know that?"

"Who? What?" Serge felt his life slipping through his fingers. "I don't know what you're talking about! Take it! Take it, I never saw anything, just don't kill me! I won't go to the cops, I swear!"

The man thumbed the safety on the pistol. "It's okay, Mr Barron. I believe you."

It was the last thing Serge ever heard.

∼

Becky let the music guide her.

It flowed through her, and she closed her eyes, no longer mouthing the words but actually singing them, belting them out loud. She strummed an imaginary guitar for the descending chords of the chorus, then threw her glass of lemonade at the wall.

She watched it spin through the air in slow motion, and noticed the wall wobble on impact.

Funny, that.

She moved her head from side to side, spinning her hands over each other like she was reeling in a fish, and danced over, turning in circles all the way until she felt pleasantly dizzy. She shoved the wall and it collapsed, revealing *more* walls, these ones white and featureless. Electrical cables twisted and looped across the floor.

She hopped away, throwing her head back and shaking her hair.

Free.

She felt *free*.

The wall opposite was the same. Becky bounded over, singing her heart out, and pushed the flimsy barrier. It fell, and there it was.

She *knew* she was being watched.

A television camera, and a clapperboard next to it that read RUMPLEJACK in neat handwriting. Against the far wall was a seating area, as if ready for a live studio audience. She looked up at the lighting rig hanging from the ceiling, then down at the floor, where the actors' marks were scrawled in white chalk.

"Not anymore," she said, and half-ran, half-danced towards the camera. It whirred relentlessly, the infinite reel of film shooting through the spools at high speed, and she knocked the camera to the ground, stomping on the lens, on the body, whacking it with the clapperboard and sending pieces of metal and plastic skittering across the bare floor. Becky snapped the camera open, tearing out handfuls of film, and ran to the bar to borrow a bottle of vodka. She spilled the contents onto the exposed film and stood before the ruined equipment, inhaling the intoxicating aroma of alcohol before producing a cigarette and lighter from her pocket. With a smile, she lit her cigarette, then set the film and camera ablaze.

"It ends here," she said, as *Disco 2000* faded out and, without missing a beat, The Sausage King segued into The Trammps' *Disco Inferno*.

She laughed as the flames licked higher, the film shrivelling and burning.

That Sausage King may be a puppet, but he was a great DJ, and a damn good dog.

~

Later, the pair of them sat on the lighthouse gallery and listened to the waves.

Becky was tired from dancing. Once she had started, she hadn't stopped. It felt like she was finally throwing off the shackles of her old life. Also, it turned out dancing was really, *really* good fun.

"Are you happy?" asked The Sausage King.

Becky fed another string of sausages into his open mouth. "All hail The Sausage King," she said, laughing at the way he ate like he'd never even *seen* a sausage before. He swallowed them with an exaggerated gulp, then leaned his round, furry head against her arm.

"Thank you for the sausages. Now, please tell me. Are you happy?"

"I am." She gazed at the horizon, where the sun was threatening to rise. "I'm happy."

"And that's the woof," said The Sausage King.

"Don't you mean the truth?"

He looked at her indignantly. "But that's what I said... and that's the woof!"

"Sure thing, Sausage King," she chuckled, and petted his head.

She gazed out over her domain, her kingdom.

It was true.

For the first time in her life, she was truly, deeply happy...

...and that's the woof.

AFTERWORD

Thank you for reading Rotten Tommy.

In this book, the character of Becky is not written as a definitive representation of autism, as that would be impossible. Autism is, of course, a spectrum. "If you've met one autistic person, you've met... *one* autistic person," as the saying goes.

If *you* are autistic, or perhaps love someone who is, you may well recognise elements of her character, while other parts may not resonate at all. As a late-diagnosed autistic person myself, I share a few traits and quirks with Becky... but certainly not all.

Lastly, please be careful if feeding your dog sausages, as store-bought, seasoned sausages can be bad for your dog's health, and even plain sausages should only be given in moderation. The Sausage King is a trained professional, and advises you not to try any of his wacky sausage-related stunts at home.

ACKNOWLEDGMENTS

Thanks to my wonderful wife Heather for her continued love and support, and for being nothing like Becky's husband.

A big shout out to the original Sausage King, Boris, for being such a goof.

Cheers to Trevor Henderson for his fabulous cover, his fourth for me!

Thumbs up to Steve Stred and Connor Corbett for keeping me sane.

Hey Anne, look — I named the cruel interrogator after you! Now stop bothering me about it.

Many thanks to Number 6 in Edinburgh.

And finally, of course, I will never tire of thanking you, dear reader, for continuing to follow me on this strange journey. I've got some wild stuff coming out in the next few years. Historical body horror, slashers, another giallo, apocalyptic action horror... and maybe even a couple of long-promised sequels.

Until then, long live truly independent horror!

Cheers,

David and Boris

MUSIC

This book was mainly written to the following bands —

Boards of Canada
Cavern of Anti-Matter
The Advisory Circle
Pye Corner Audio
Space
Space Art

My writing playlist is pinned to my Spotify profile, so if you want to give it a listen, find me over there. There's a link at the bottom of my official website.

ABOUT THE AUTHOR

David Sodergren lives in Scotland with his wife Heather and his best friend, Boris the Pug.

Growing up, he was the kind of kid who collected rubber skeletons and lived for horror movies.

Not much has changed since then.

Since the publication of his first novel, The Forgotten Island, he has written and published a further nine novels, from slashers to gialli to folk horror to weird westerns to bikersploitation to romantic horror.

𝕏 x.com/paperbacksnpugs
⌾ instagram.com/paperbacksandpugs

ALSO BY DAVID SODERGREN

THE FORGOTTEN ISLAND

NIGHT SHOOT

DEAD GIRL BLUES

MAGGIE'S GRAVE

THE NAVAJO NIGHTMARE (with Steve Stred)

THE PERFECT VICTIM

SATAN'S BURNOUTS MUST DIE!

THE HAAR

AND BY GOD'S HAND YOU SHALL DIE

HEX-PERIMENTS: A DARK BIOTECH ANTHOLOGY

(featuring the story 'Those Damn Trees')

THE HORROR COLLECTION: SAPPHIRE EDITION

(featuring the story 'The Upstairs Neighbour')